GENE LUEN YANG
& MIKE HOLMES

PH CASS COUNTY PUBLIC LIBRARY
400 E. MECHANIC
HARRISONVILLE, MO 64701

First Second

New York

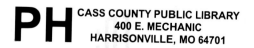

First Second

New York

Copyright © 2015 by Humble Comics LLC

Published by First Second
First Second is an imprint of Roaring Brook Press,
a division of Holtzbrinck Publishing Holdings Limited Partnership
175 Fifth Avenue, New York, New York 10010

Cataloging-in-Publication Data is on file at the Library of Congress

Paperback ISBN: 978-1-62672-075-6
Hardcover ISBN: 978-1-62672-276-7

First Second books may be purchased for business or promotional use.
For information on bulk purchases please contact Macmillan Corporate
and Premium Sales Department at (800) 221-7945 x5442 or by email at
specialmarkets@macmillan.com.

FIRST
EDITION

First edition 2015

Book design by Rob Steen

Printed in China by Toppan Leefung Printing Ltd., Dongguan City, Guangdong Province

Paperback: 10 9 8 7 6 5
Hardcover: 10 9 8 7 6 5 4 3 2

"It was this wonderful time between magic and so-called rationality."

–Wally Feurzeig, co-creator of the Logo programming language, on the early days of Logo

Chapter

Listen.

I'm going to tell
you a story--

--a story about *me*.

But I'm telling you so
you'll remember--

--remember about *you*.

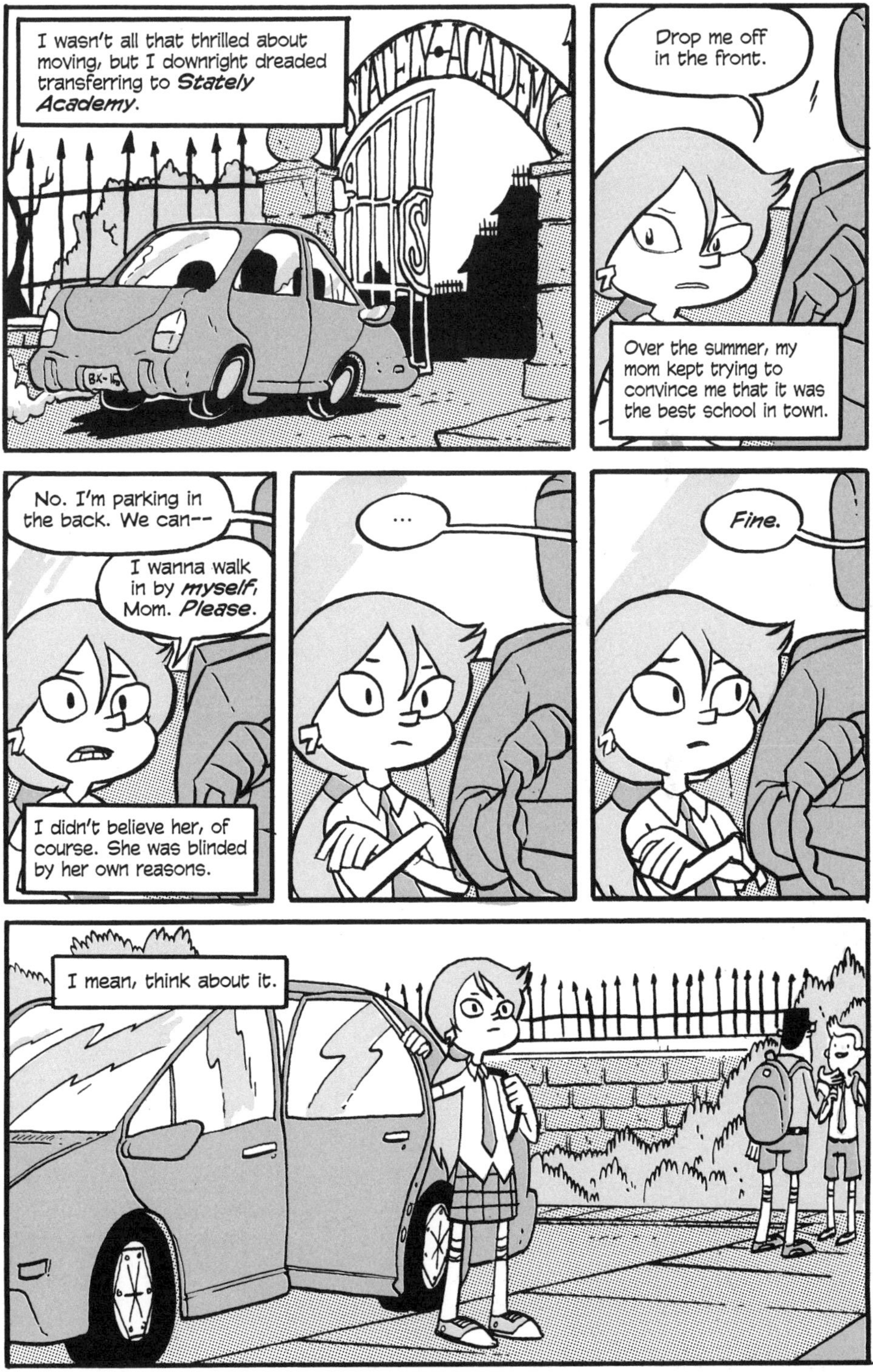
I wasn't all that thrilled about moving, but I downright dreaded transferring to *Stately Academy*.
STATELY ACADEMY
Drop me off in the front.
Over the summer, my mom kept trying to convince me that it was the best school in town.
No. I'm parking in the back. We can--
I wanna walk in by *myself*, Mom. *Please*.
I didn't believe her, of course. She was blinded by her own reasons.
...
Fine.
I mean, think about it.

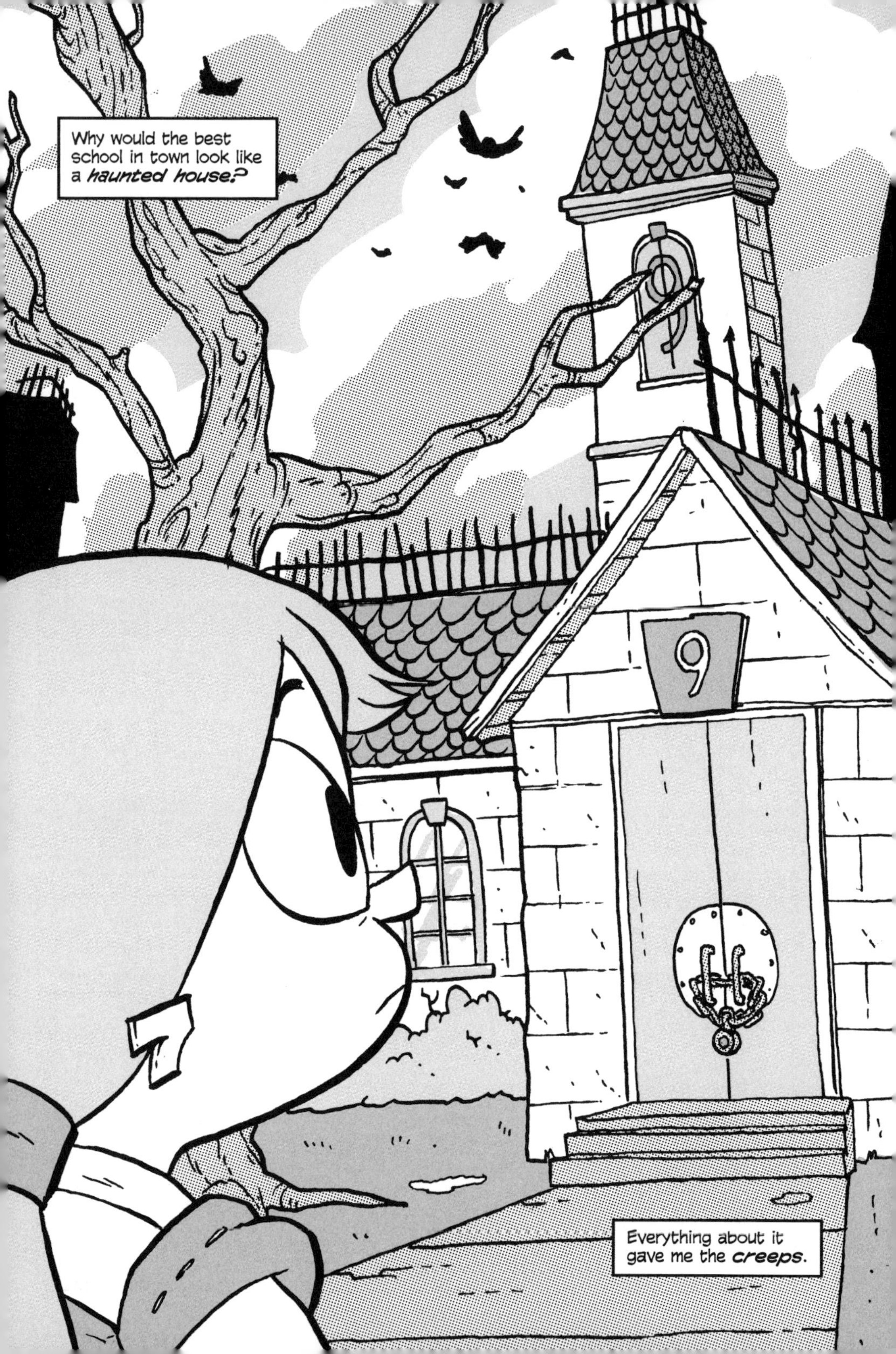
Why would the best school in town look like a *haunted house?*
9
Everything about it gave me the *creeps*.

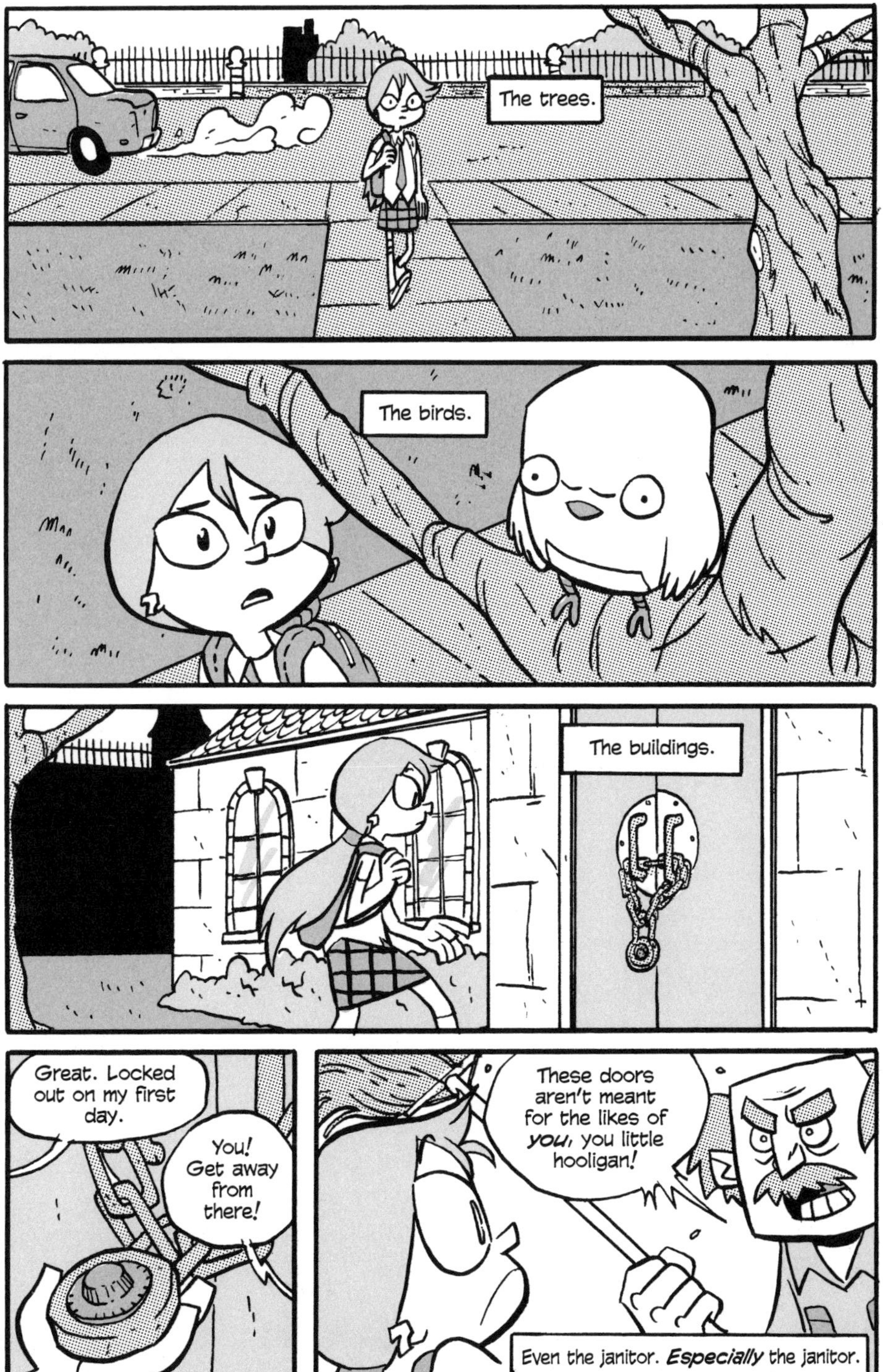
The trees.
The birds.
The buildings.
Great. Locked out on my first day.
You! Get away from there!
These doors aren't meant for the likes of *you*, you little hooligan!
Even the janitor. ***Especially*** the janitor.

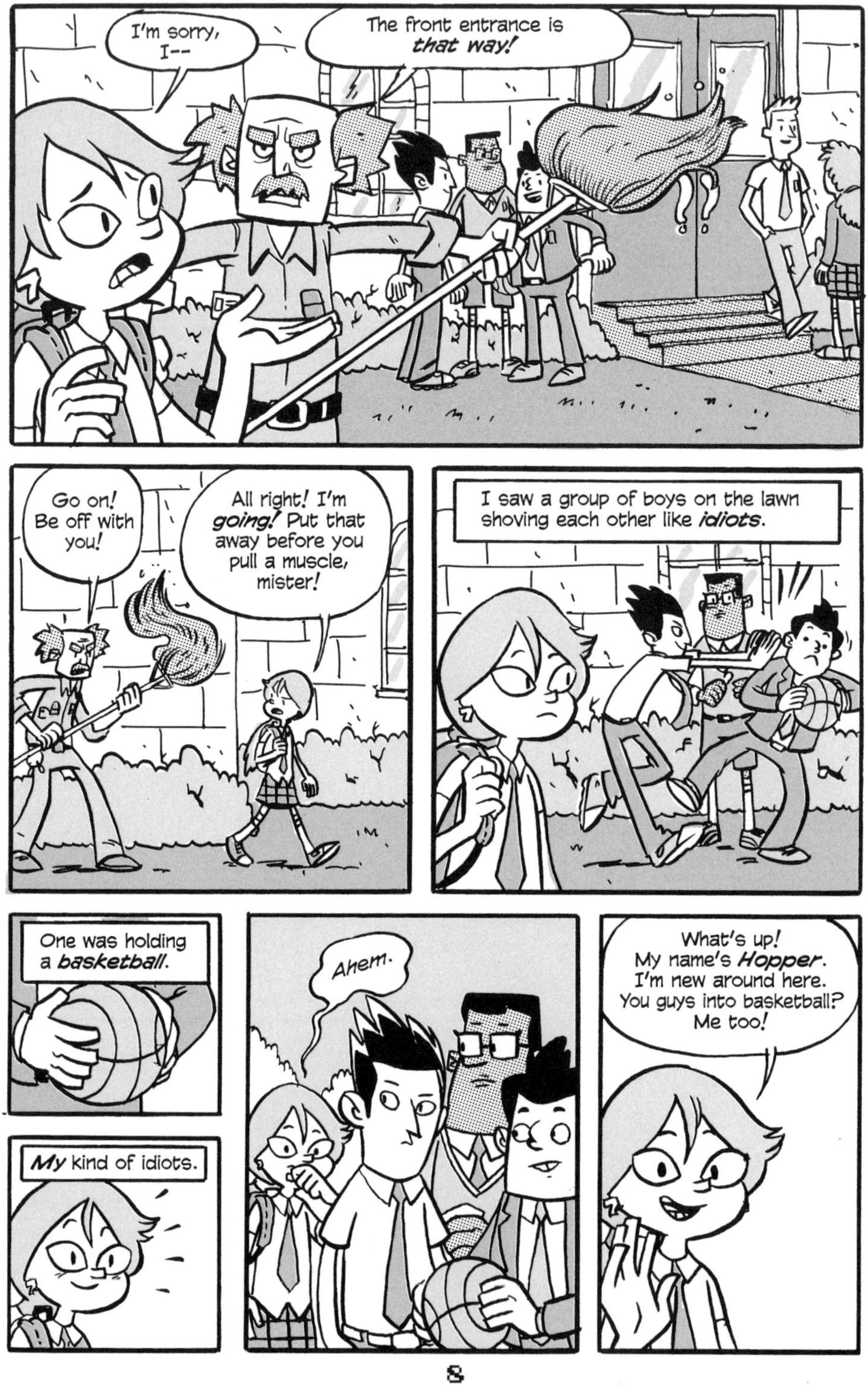
I'm sorry, I--
The front entrance is *that way!*
Go on! Be off with you!
All right! I'm *going!* Put that away before you pull a muscle, mister!
I saw a group of boys on the lawn shoving each other like *idiots*.
One was holding a *basketball*.
My kind of idiots.
Ahem.
What's up! My name's *Hopper*. I'm new around here. You guys into basketball? Me too!

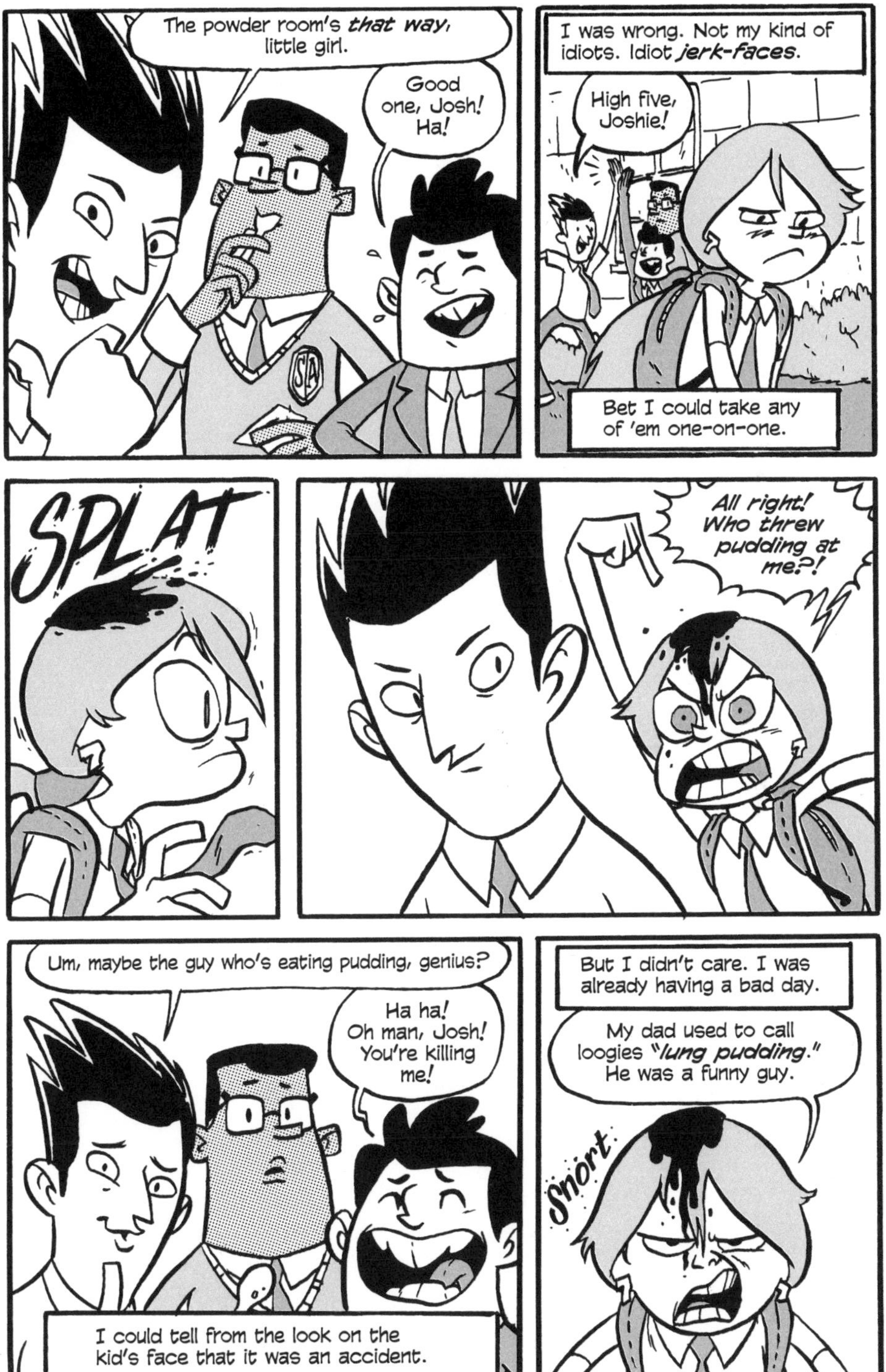

The powder room's *that way,* little girl.
Good one, Josh! Ha!
I was wrong. Not my kind of idiots. Idiot *jerk-faces*.
High five, Joshie!
Bet I could take any of 'em one-on-one.
SPLAT
All right! Who threw pudding at me?!
Um, maybe the guy who's eating pudding, genius?
Ha ha! Oh man, Josh! You're killing me!
I could tell from the look on the kid's face that it was an accident.
But I didn't care. I was already having a bad day.
My dad used to call loogies "*lung pudding*." He was a funny guy.
Snort

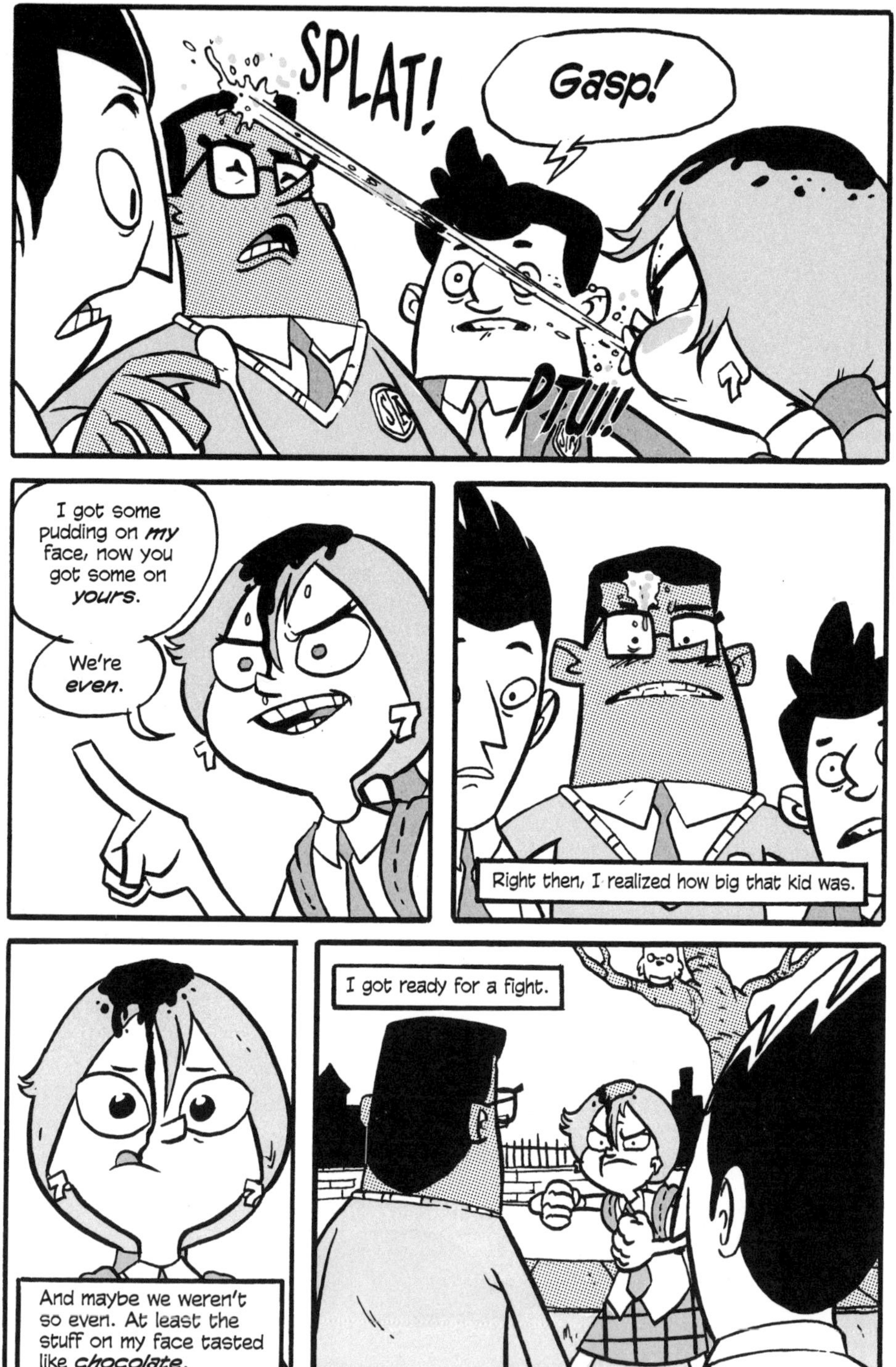
SPLAT!
Gasp!
PTUI!
I got some pudding on *my* face, now you got some on *yours*.
We're *even*.
Right then, I realized how big that kid was.
And maybe we weren't so even. At least the stuff on my face tasted like *chocolate*.
I got ready for a fight.

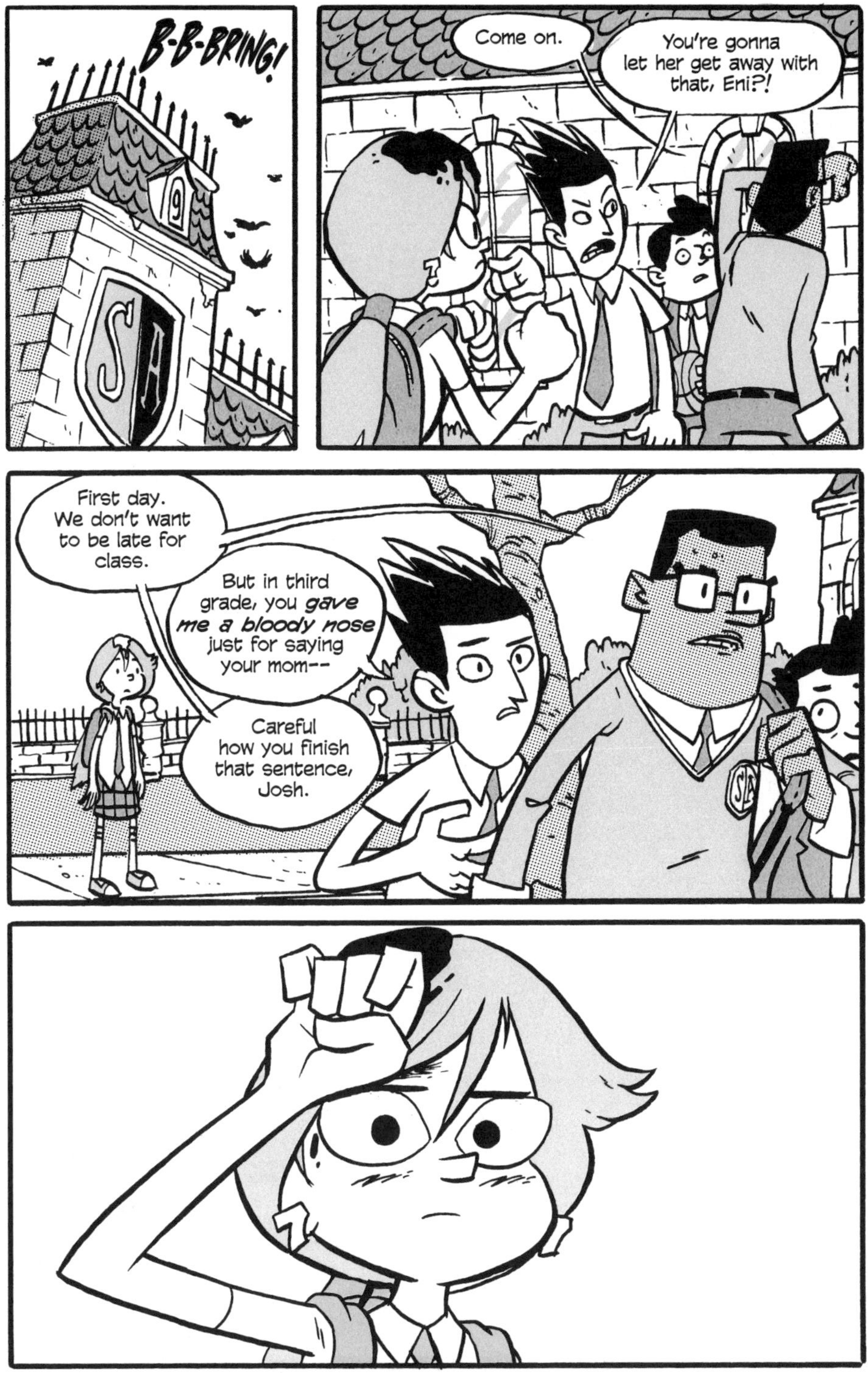
B-B-BRING!
Come on.
You're gonna let her get away with that, Eni?!
First day. We don't want to be late for class.
But in third grade, you *gave me a bloody nose* just for saying your mom--
Careful how you finish that sentence, Josh.

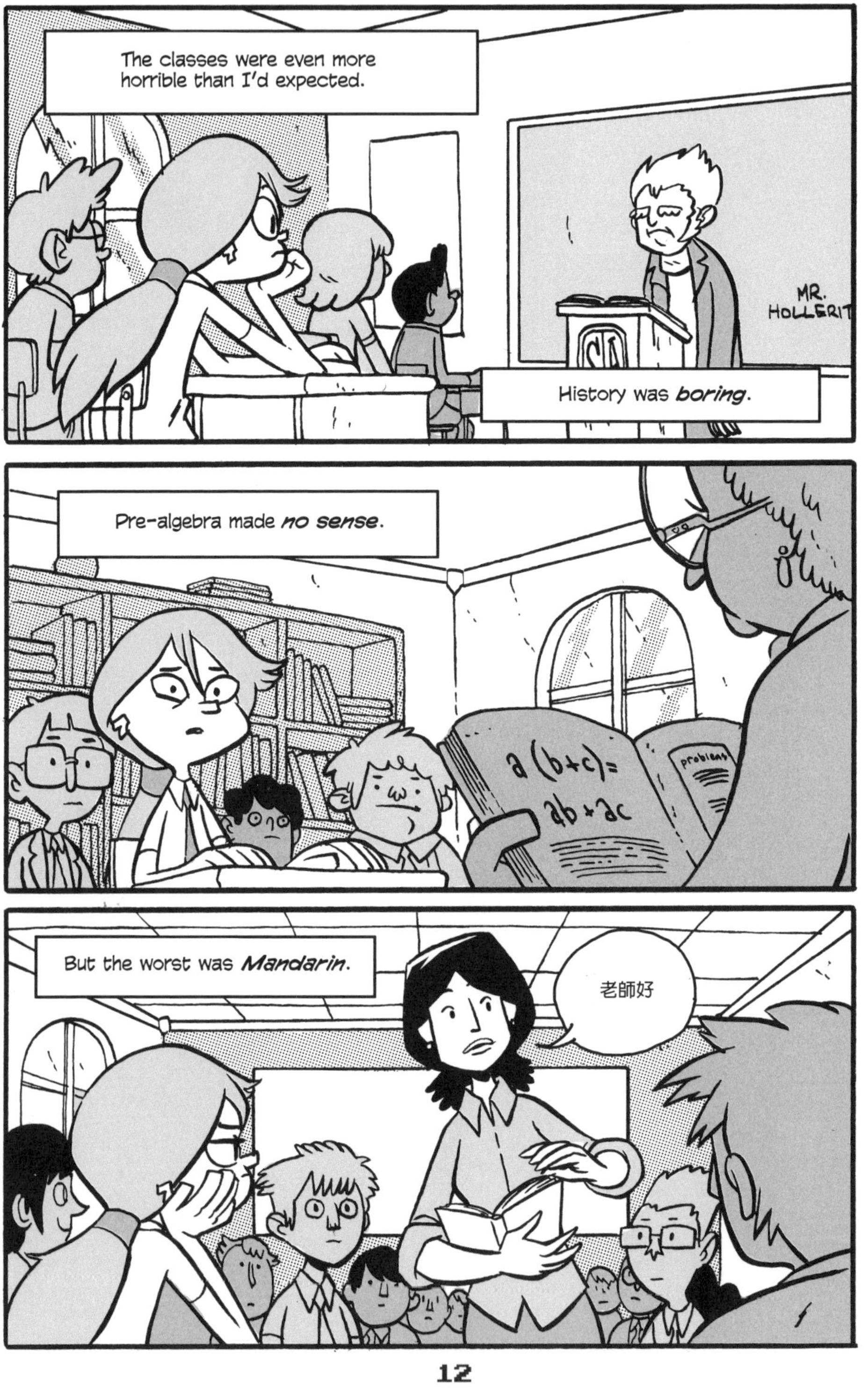
The classes were even more horrible than I'd expected.
MR. HOLLERIT
History was *boring*.
Pre-algebra made *no sense*.
a (b+c)= ab+ac
But the worst was *Mandarin*.
老師好

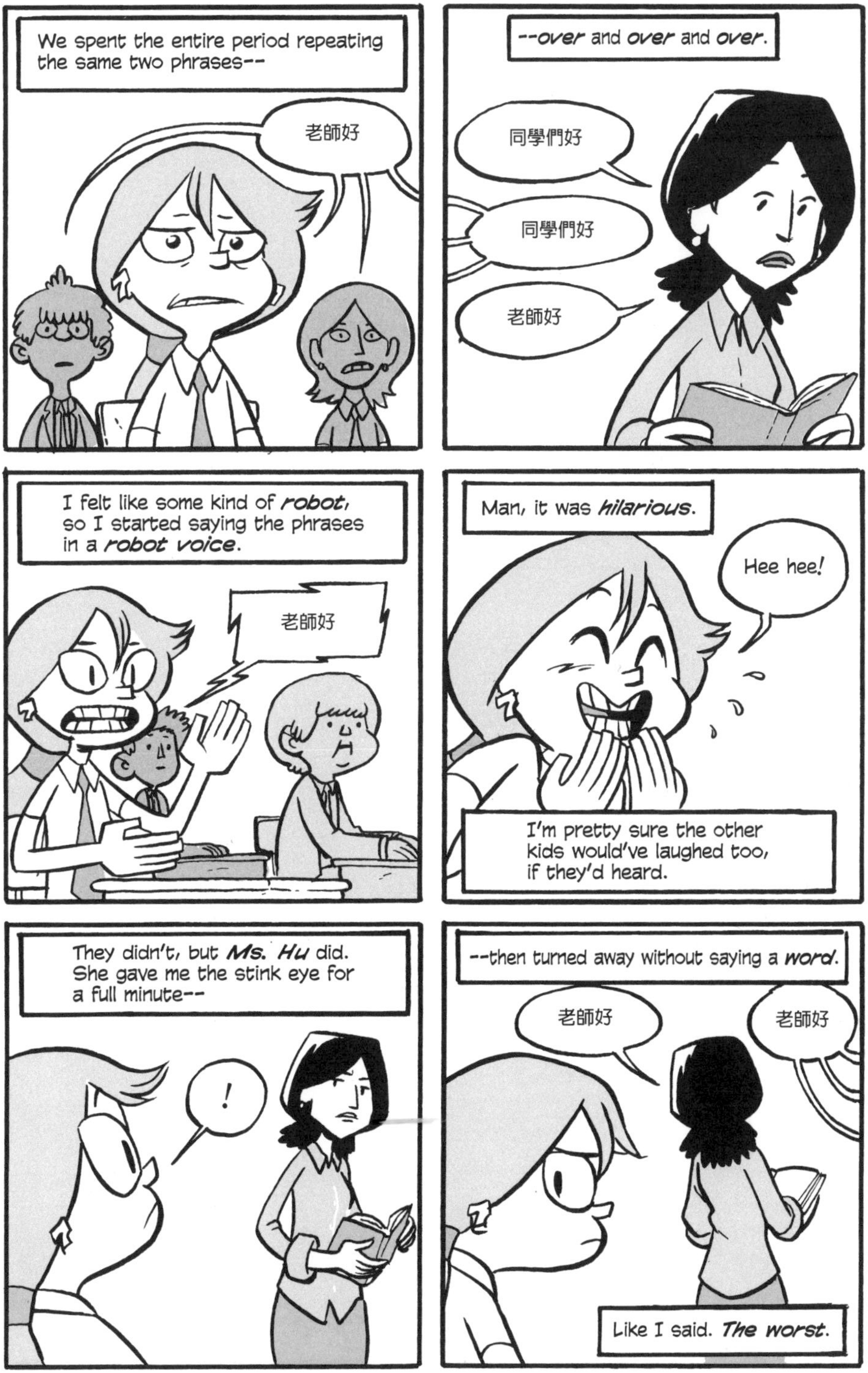
We spent the entire period repeating the same two phrases--
老師好
--over and over and over.
同學們好
同學們好
老師好
I felt like some kind of robot, so I started saying the phrases in a robot voice.
老師好
Man, it was hilarious.
Hee hee!
I'm pretty sure the other kids would've laughed too, if they'd heard.
They didn't, but Ms. Hu did. She gave me the stink eye for a full minute--
!
--then turned away without saying a word.
老師好
老師好
Like I said. The worst.

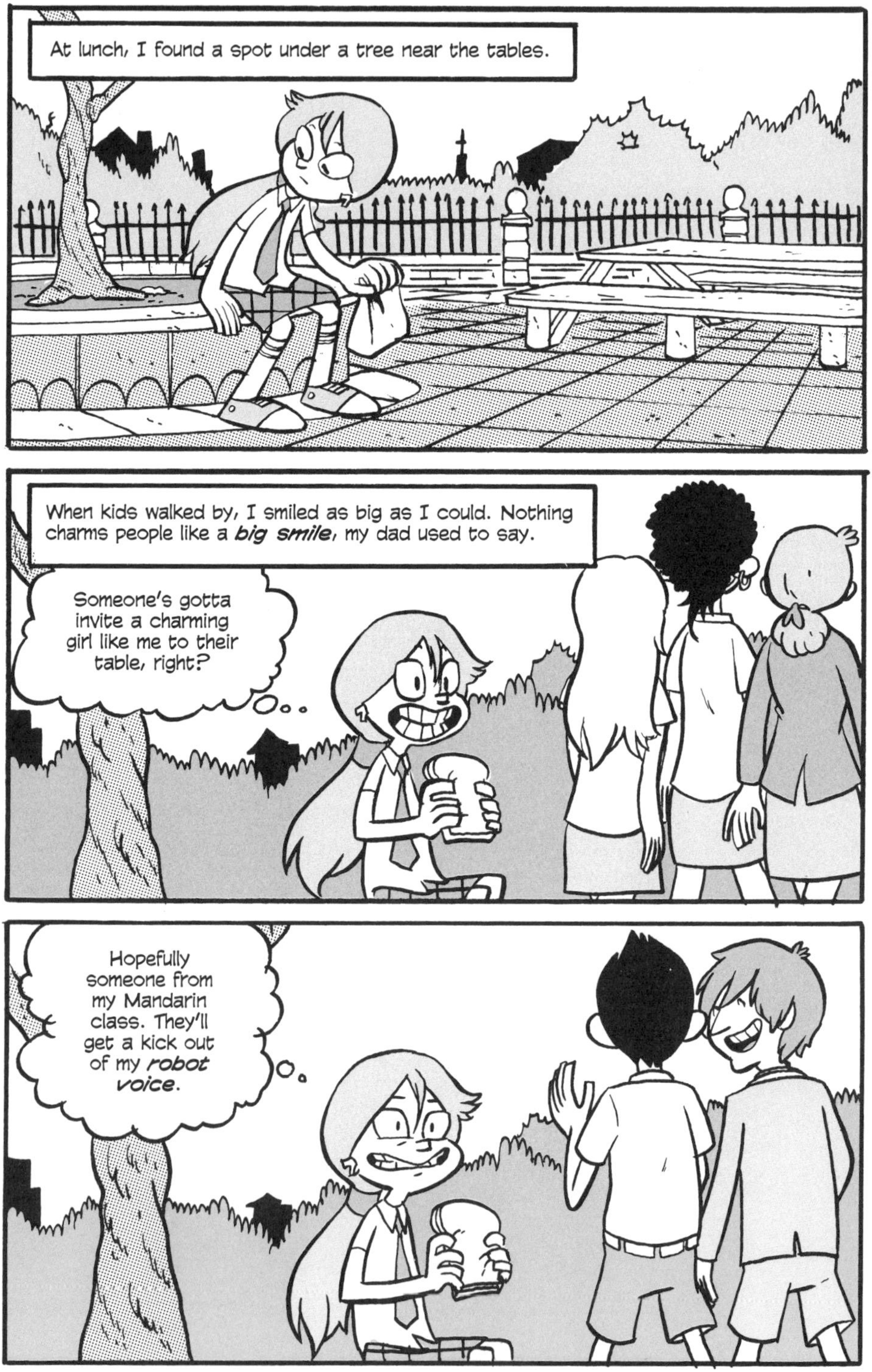
At lunch, I found a spot under a tree near the tables.
When kids walked by, I smiled as big as I could. Nothing charms people like a *big smile*, my dad used to say.
Someone's gotta invite a charming girl like me to their table, right?
Hopefully someone from my Mandarin class. They'll get a kick out of my *robot voice*.

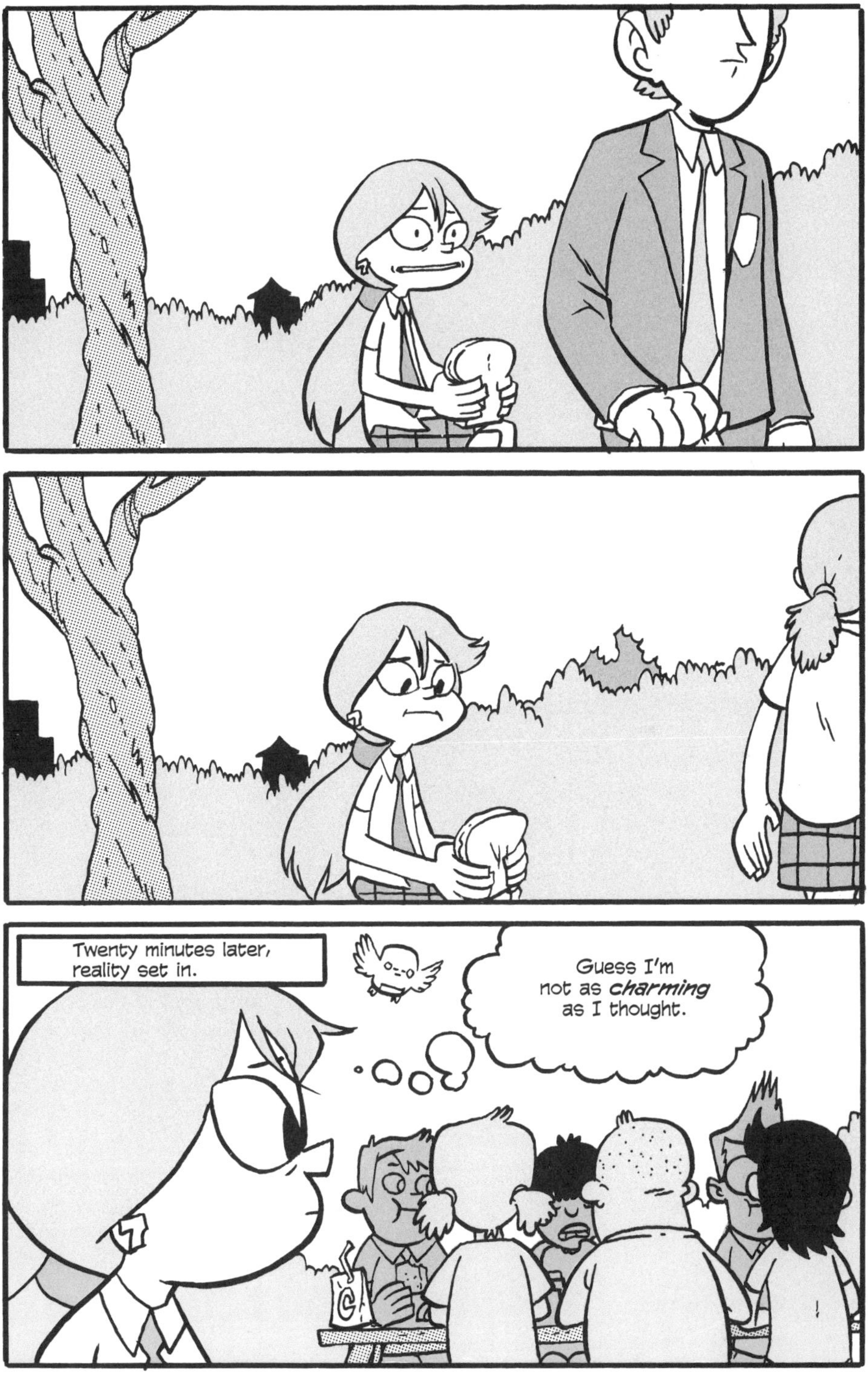
Twenty minutes later, reality set in.
Guess I'm not as *charming* as I thought.

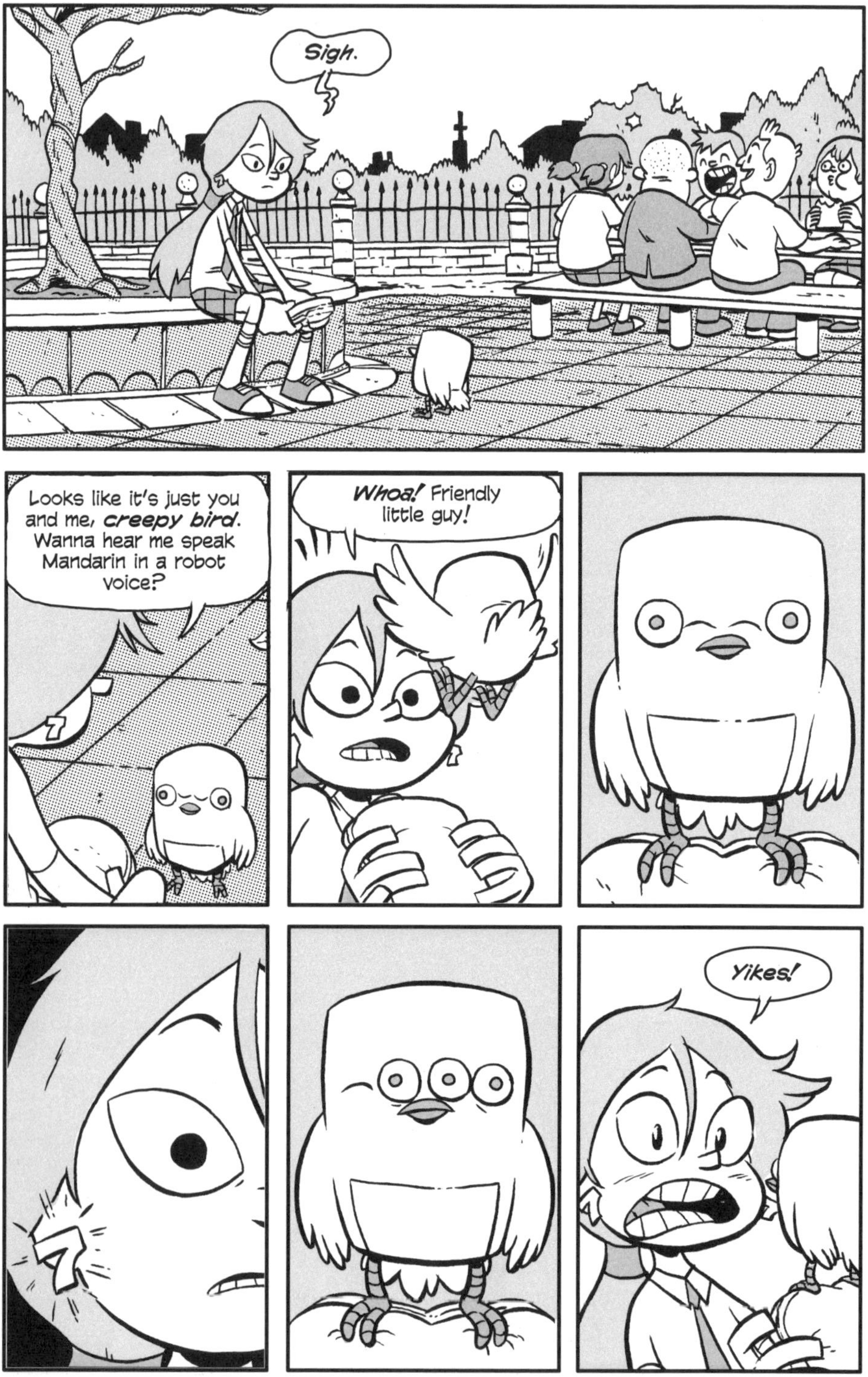
Sigh.
Looks like it's just you and me, *creepy bird*. Wanna hear me speak Mandarin in a robot voice?
Whoa! Friendly little guy!
Yikes!

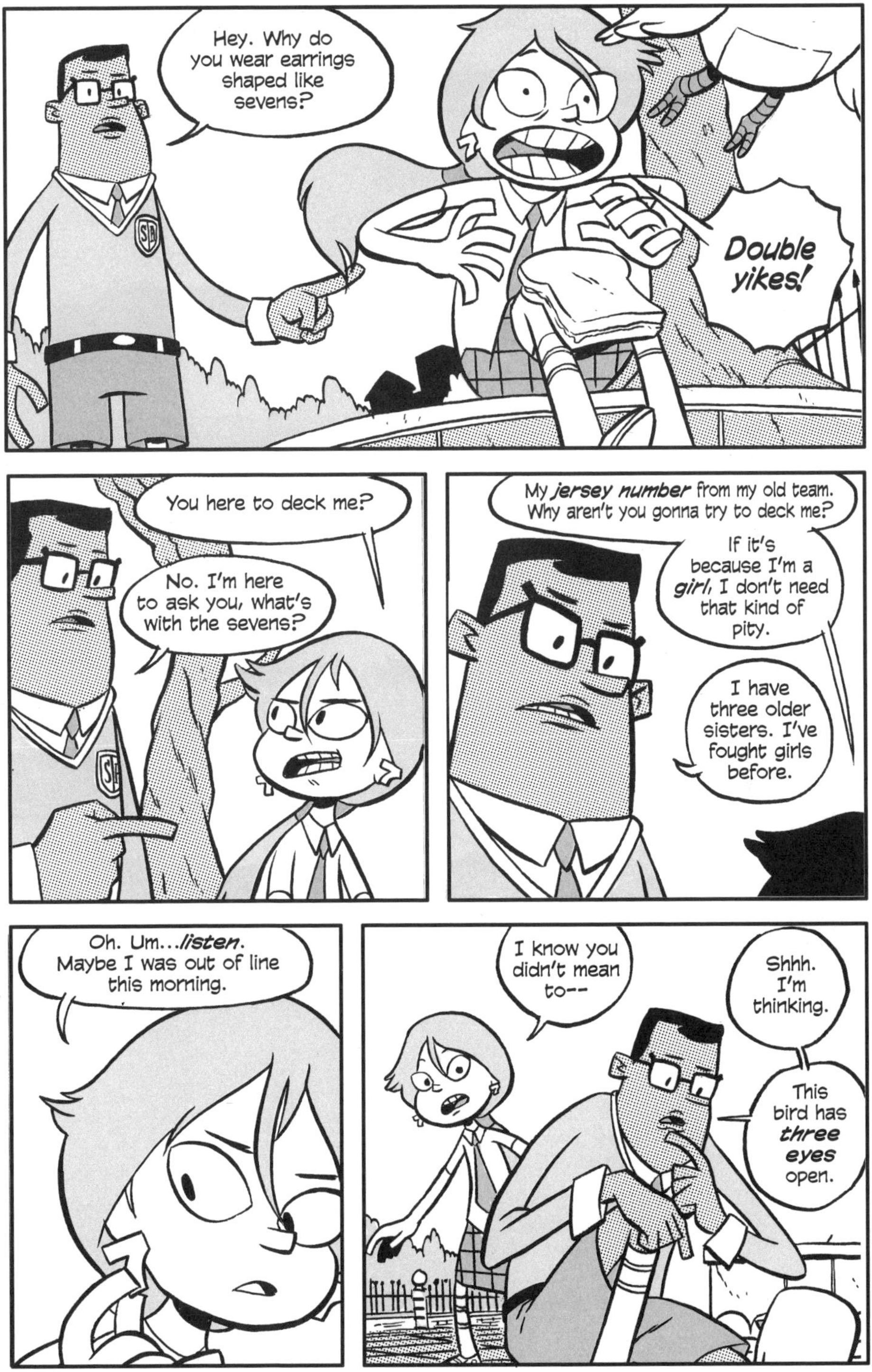
Hey. Why do you wear earrings shaped like sevens?
Double yikes!
You here to deck me?
No. I'm here to ask you, what's with the sevens?
My *jersey number* from my old team. Why aren't you gonna try to deck me?
If it's because I'm a *girl*, I don't need that kind of pity.
I have three older sisters. I've fought girls before.
Oh. Um...*listen*. Maybe I was out of line this morning.
I know you didn't mean to--
Shhh. I'm thinking.
This bird has **three eyes** open.

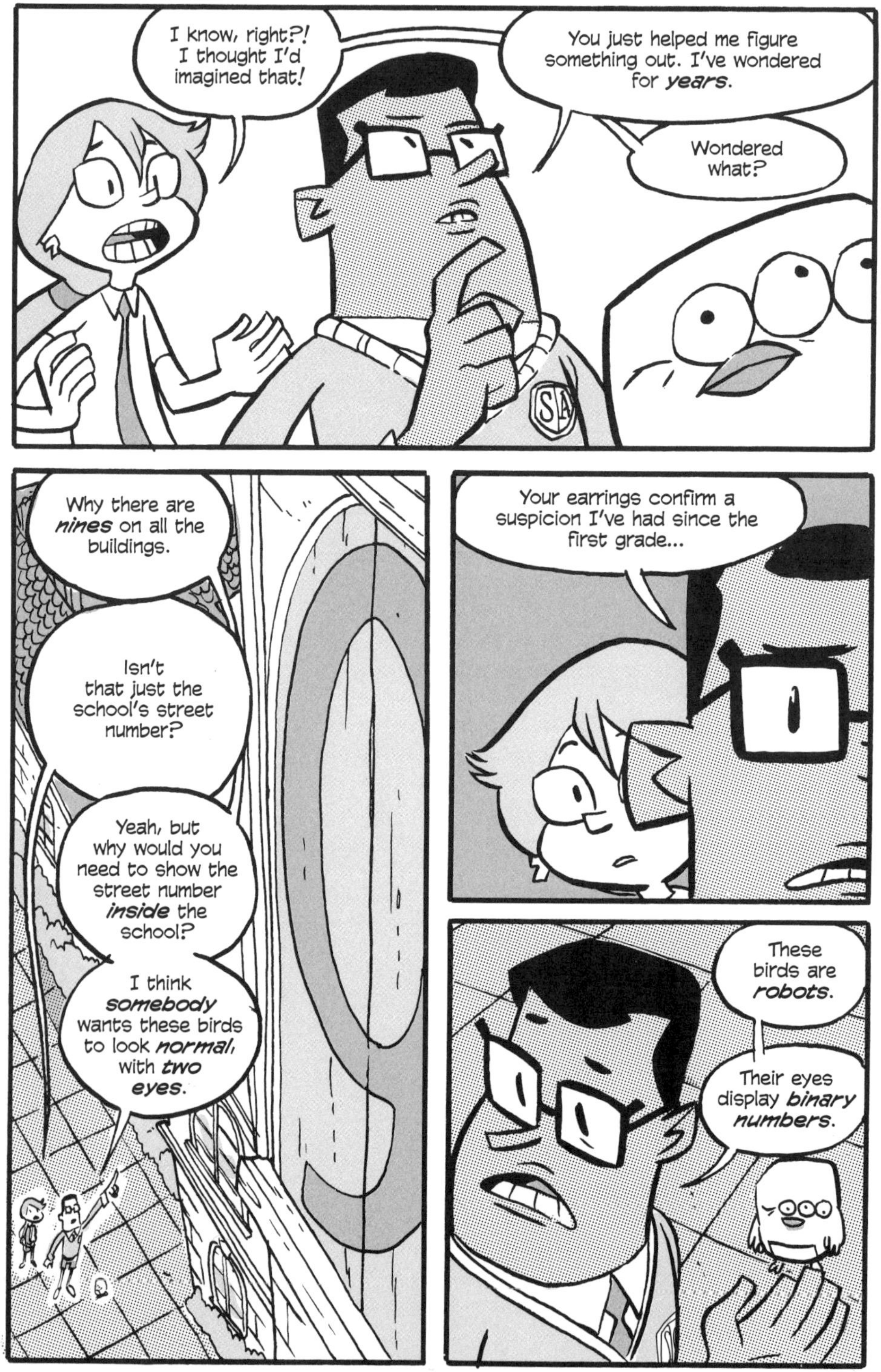

I know, right?! I thought I'd imagined that!
You just helped me figure something out. I've wondered for *years*.
Wondered what?
Why there are *nines* on all the buildings.
Isn't that just the school's street number?
Yeah, but why would you need to show the street number *inside* the school?
I think *somebody* wants these birds to look *normal*, with *two eyes*.
Your earrings confirm a suspicion I've had since the first grade...
These birds are *robots*.
Their eyes display *binary numbers*.

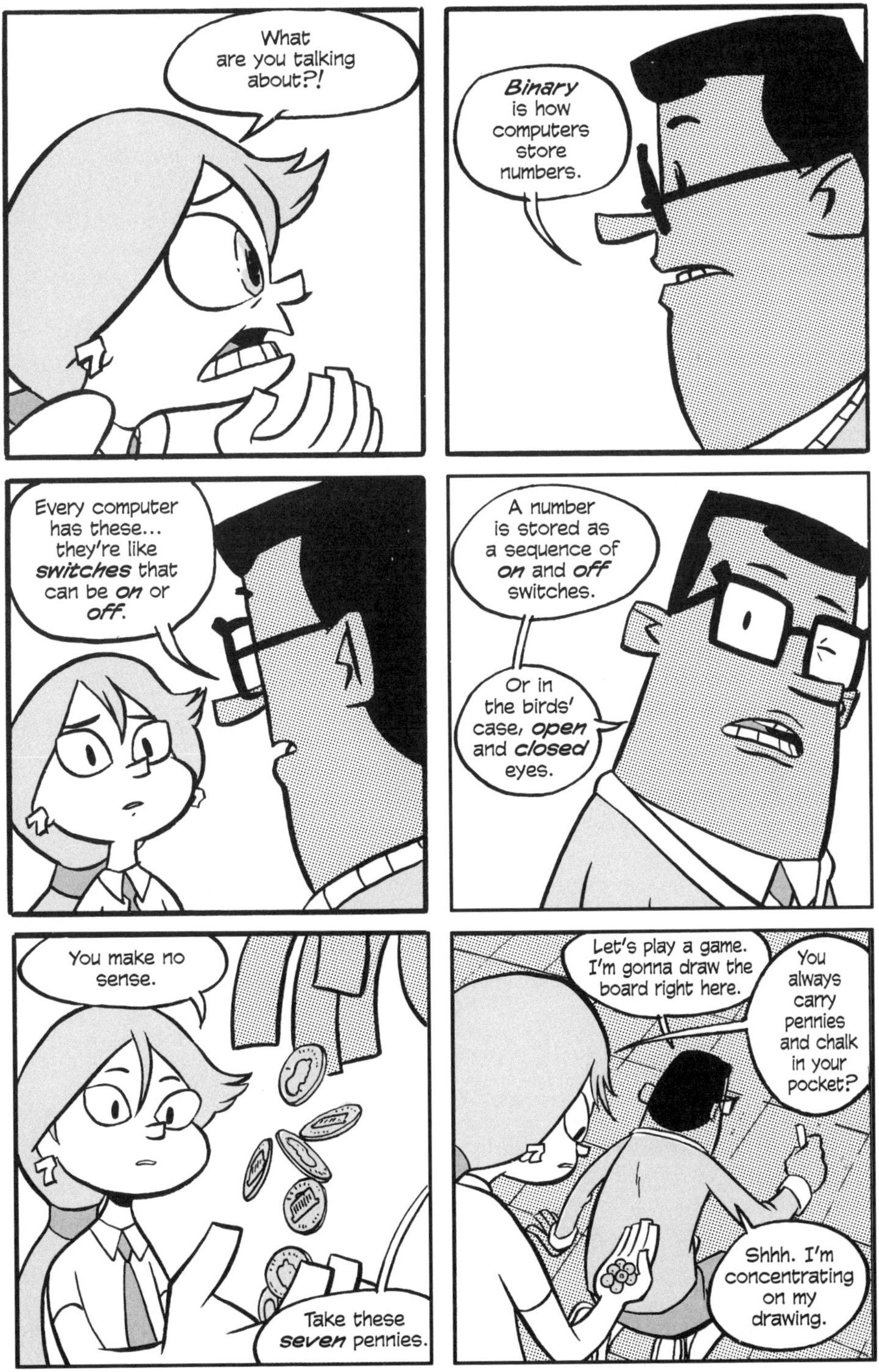
What are you talking about?!
Binary is how computers store numbers.
Every computer has these... they're like switches that can be on or off.
A number is stored as a sequence of on and off switches.
Or in the birds' case, open and closed eyes.
You make no sense.
Take these seven pennies.
Let's play a game. I'm gonna draw the board right here.
You always carry pennies and chalk in your pocket?
Shhh. I'm concentrating on my drawing.

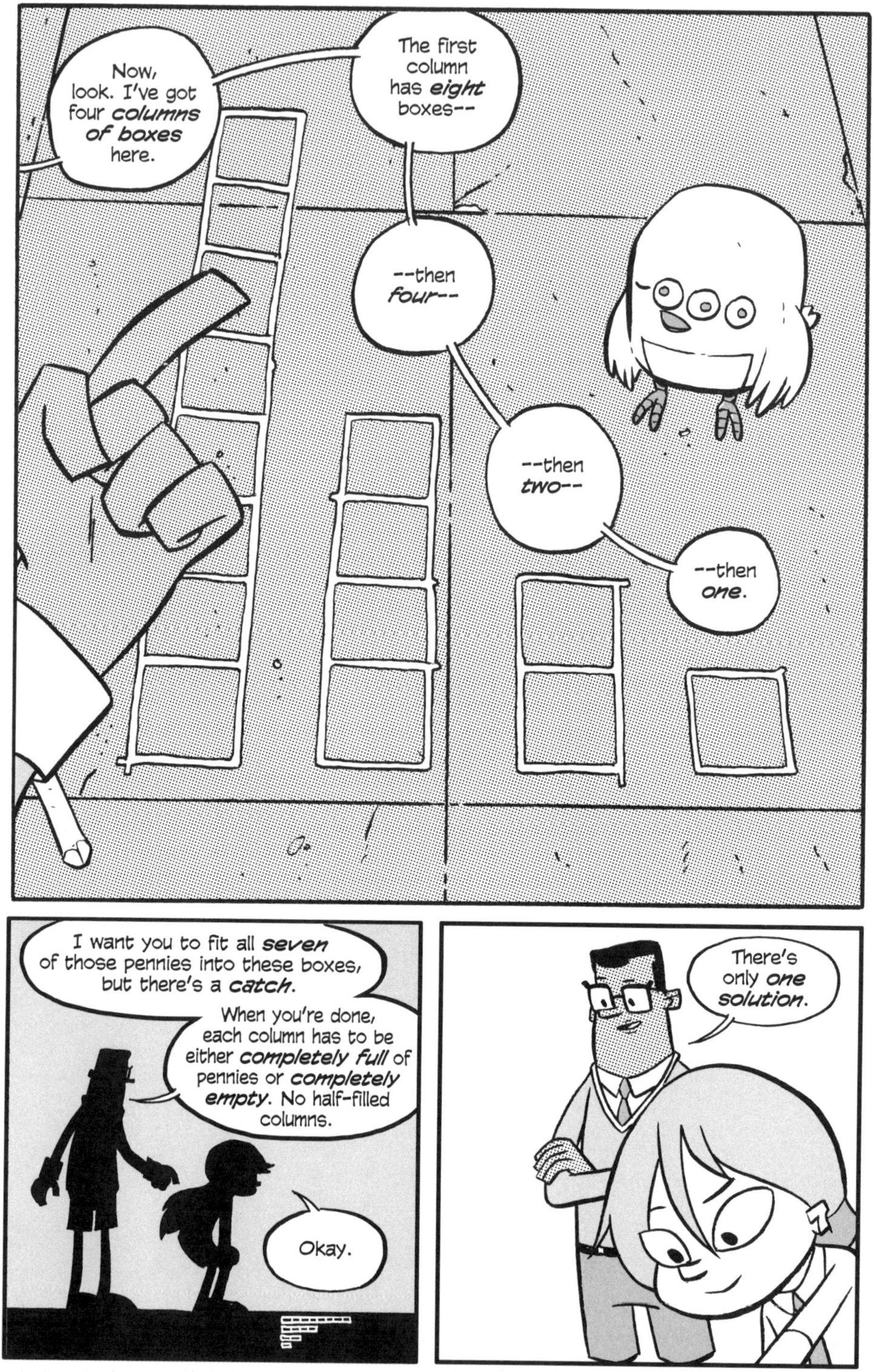
Now, look. I've got four columns of boxes here.
The first column has eight boxes--
--then four--
--then two--
--then one.
I want you to fit all seven of those pennies into these boxes, but there's a catch.
When you're done, each column has to be either completely full of pennies or completely empty. No half-filled columns.
Okay.
There's only one solution.

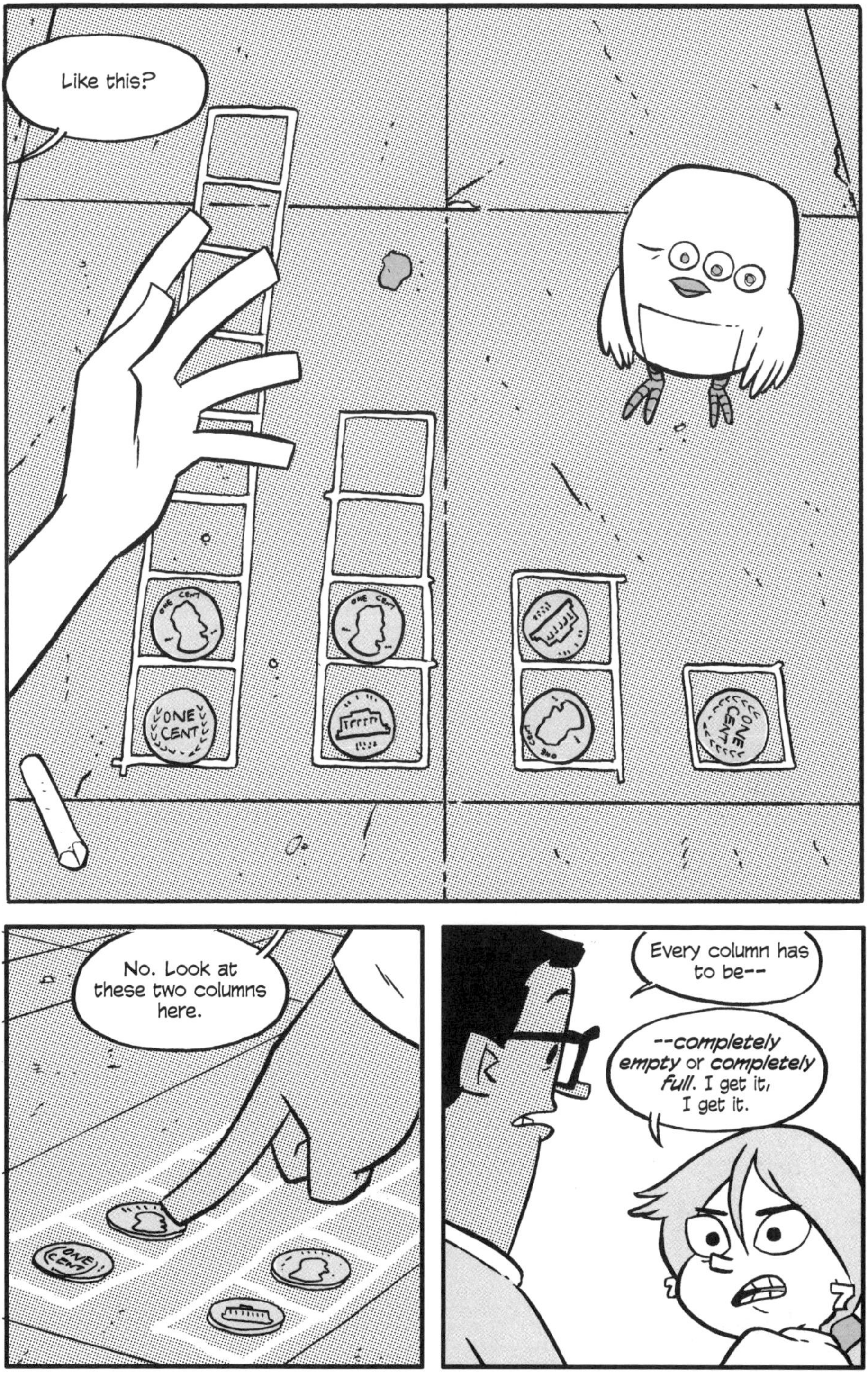
Like this?
No. Look at these two columns here.
Every column has to be--
--*completely empty* or *completely full*. I get it, I get it.
ONE CENT

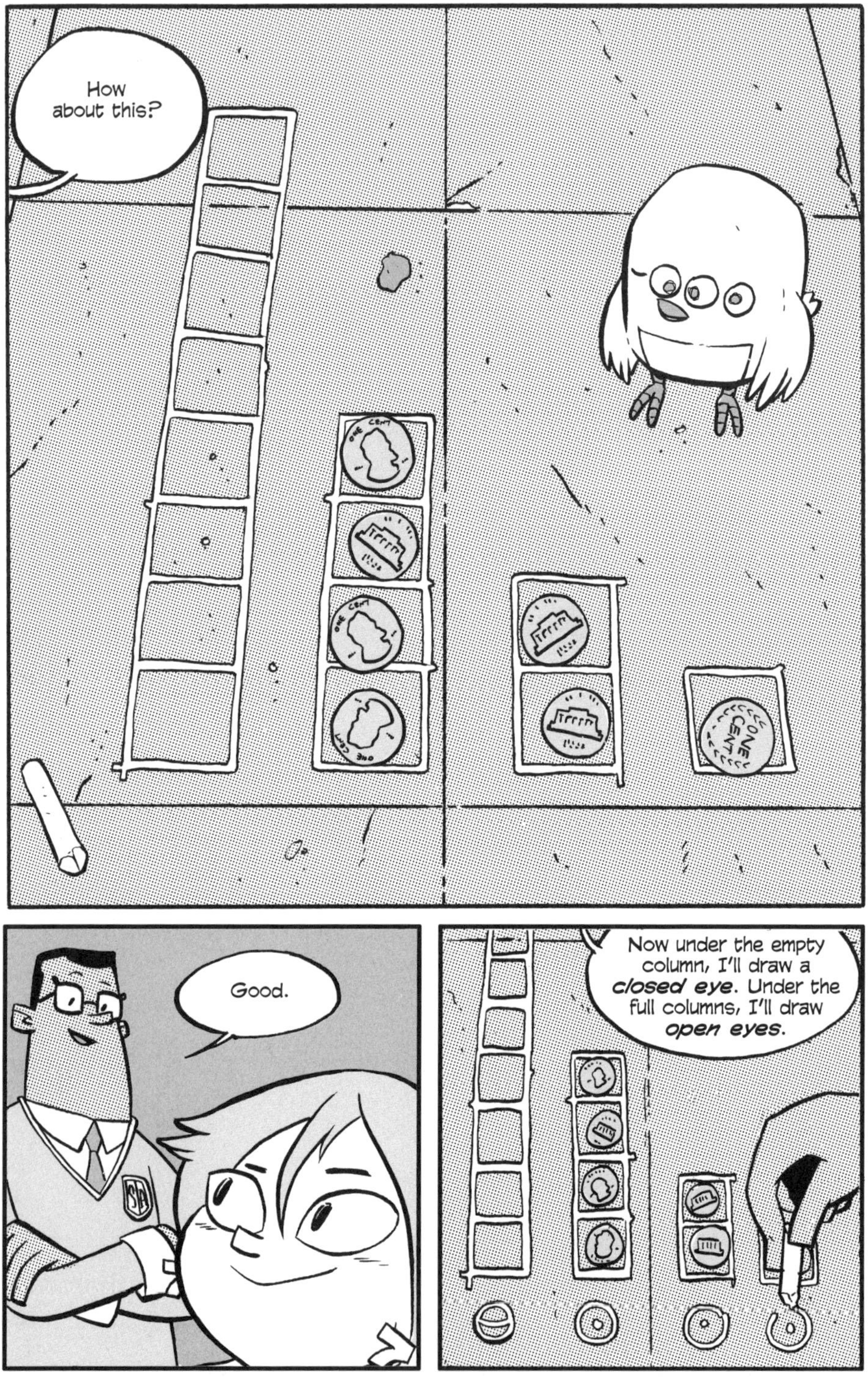
How about this?
Good.
Now under the empty column, I'll draw a ***closed eye***. Under the full columns, I'll draw ***open eyes***.

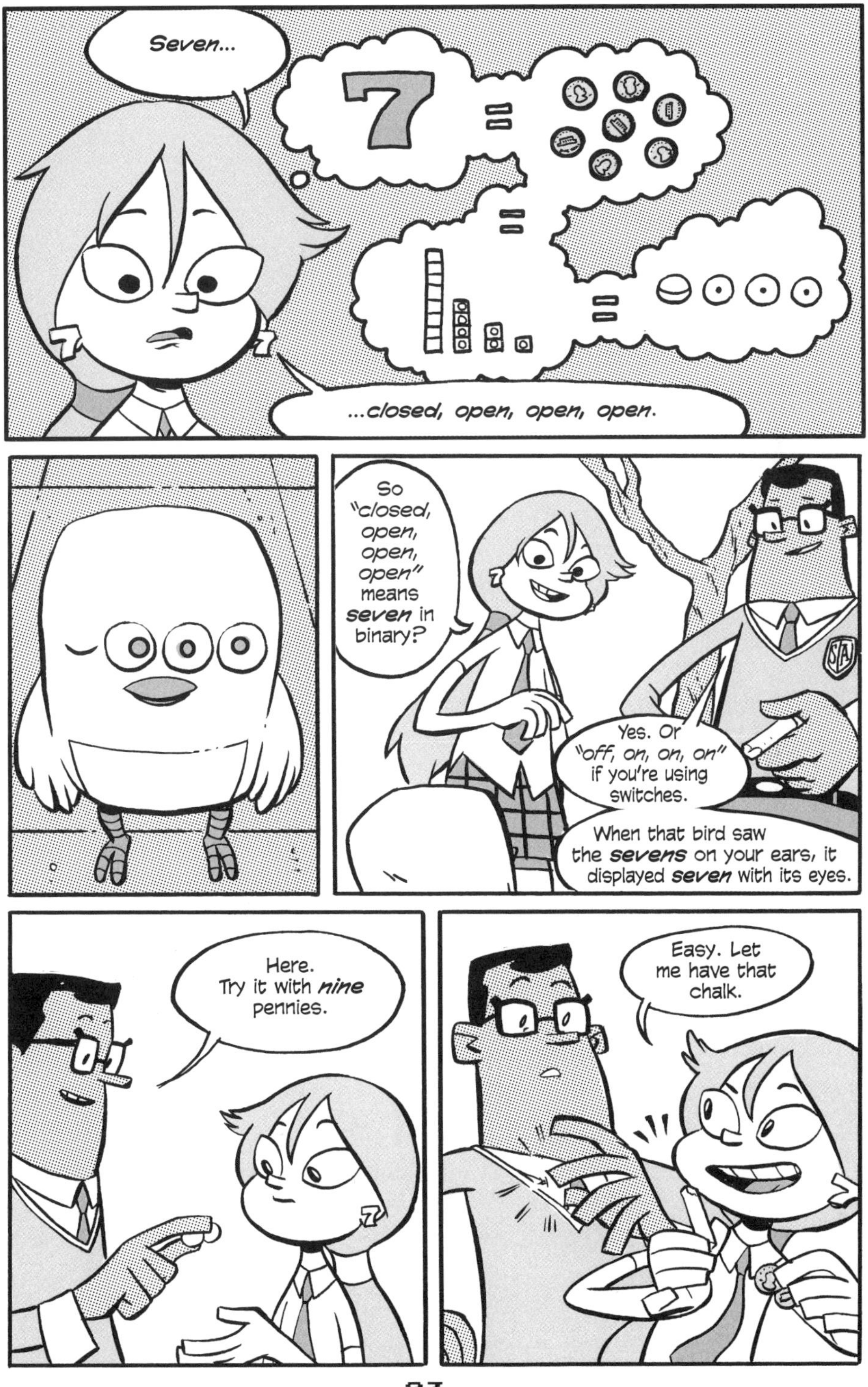

Seven...
7 = = =
...closed, open, open, open.
So "closed, open, open, open" means seven in binary?
Yes. Or "off, on, on, on" if you're using switches.
When that bird saw the sevens on your ears, it displayed seven with its eyes.
Here. Try it with nine pennies.
Easy. Let me have that chalk.

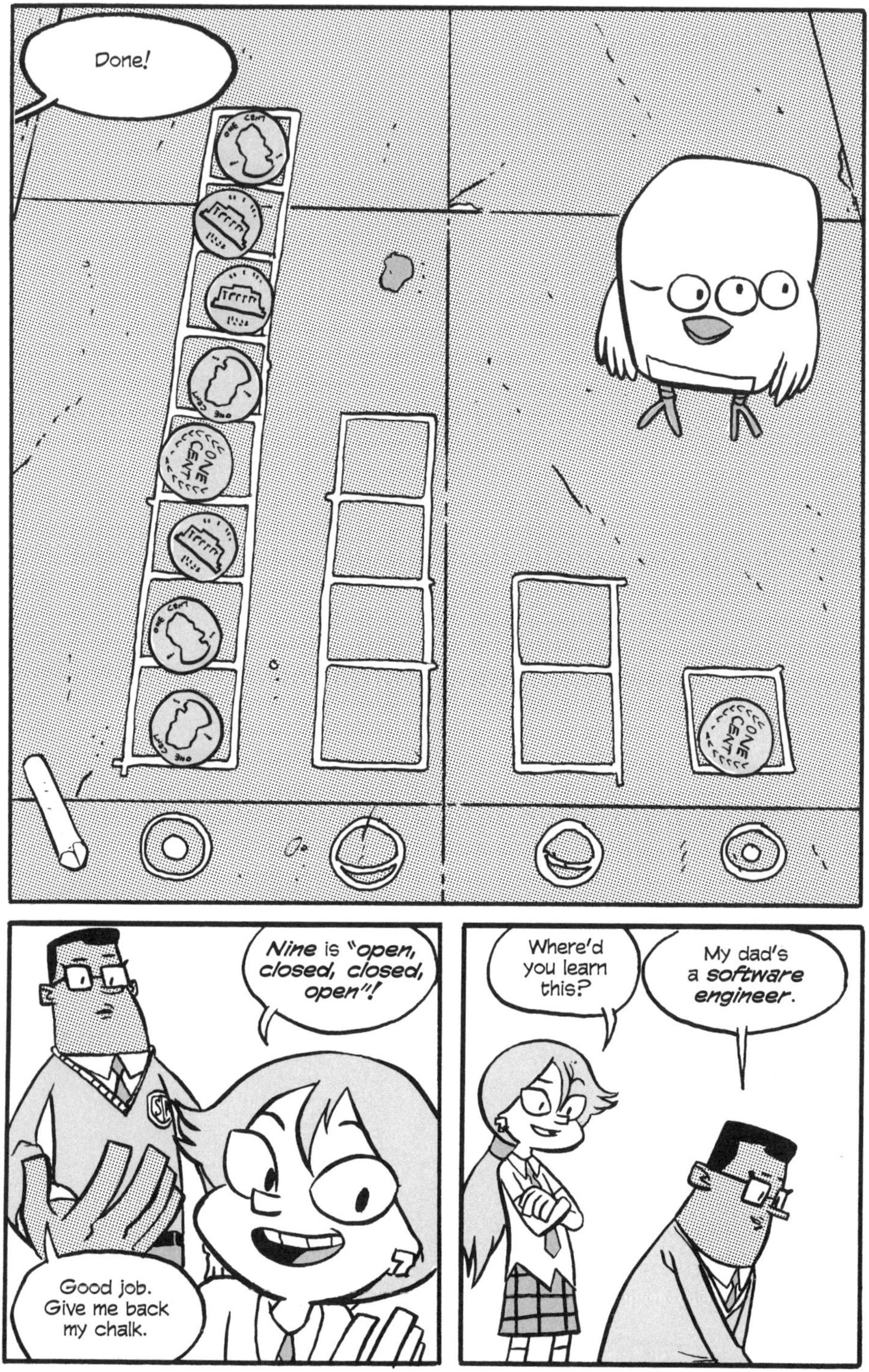
Done!
Nine is "open, closed, closed, open"!
Good job. Give me back my chalk.
Where'd you learn this?
My dad's a software engineer.

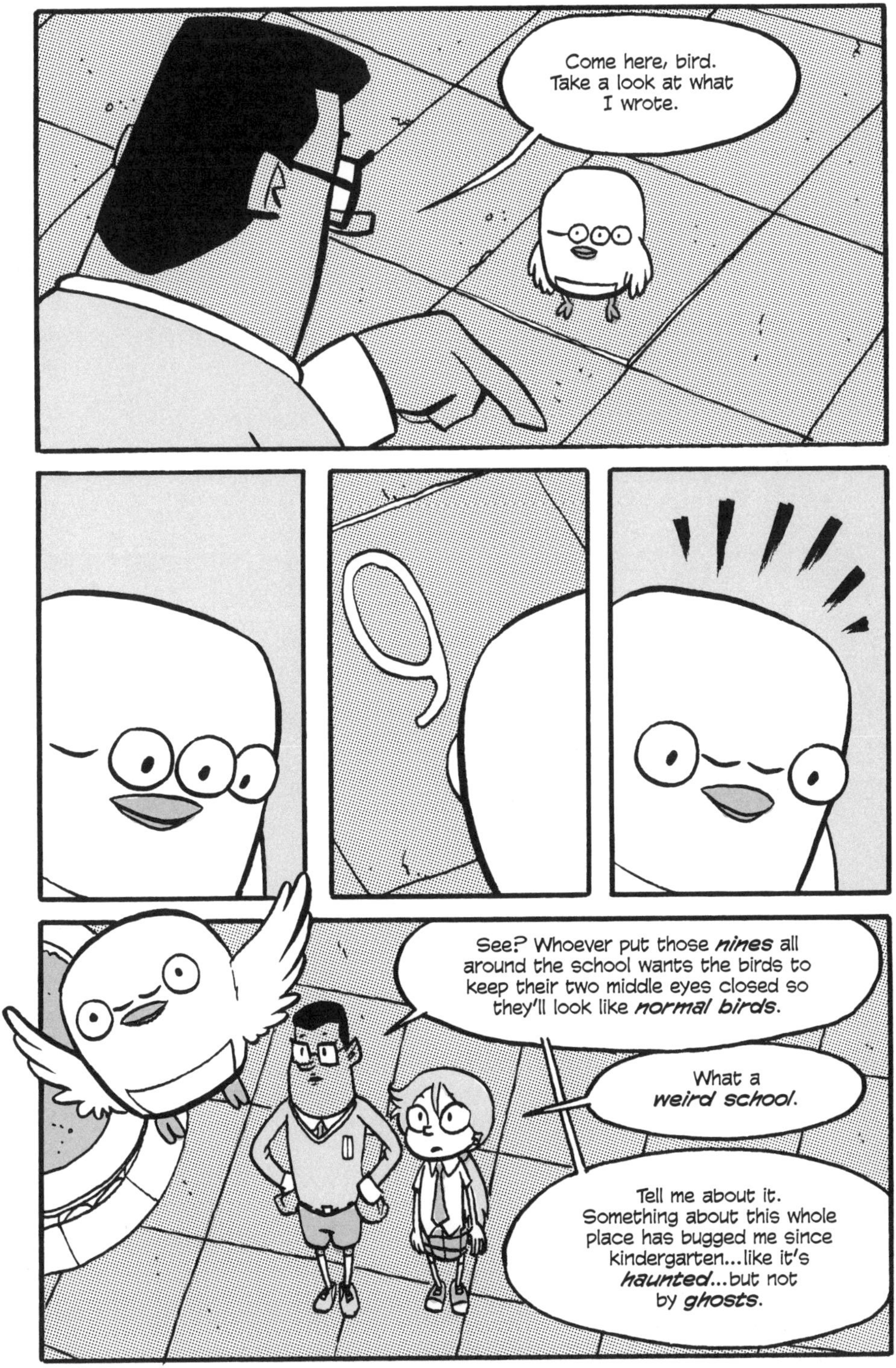
Come here, bird. Take a look at what I wrote.
See? Whoever put those *nines* all around the school wants the birds to keep their two middle eyes closed so they'll look like *normal birds*.
What a *weird school*.
Tell me about it. Something about this whole place has bugged me since kindergarten...like it's *haunted*...but not by *ghosts*.

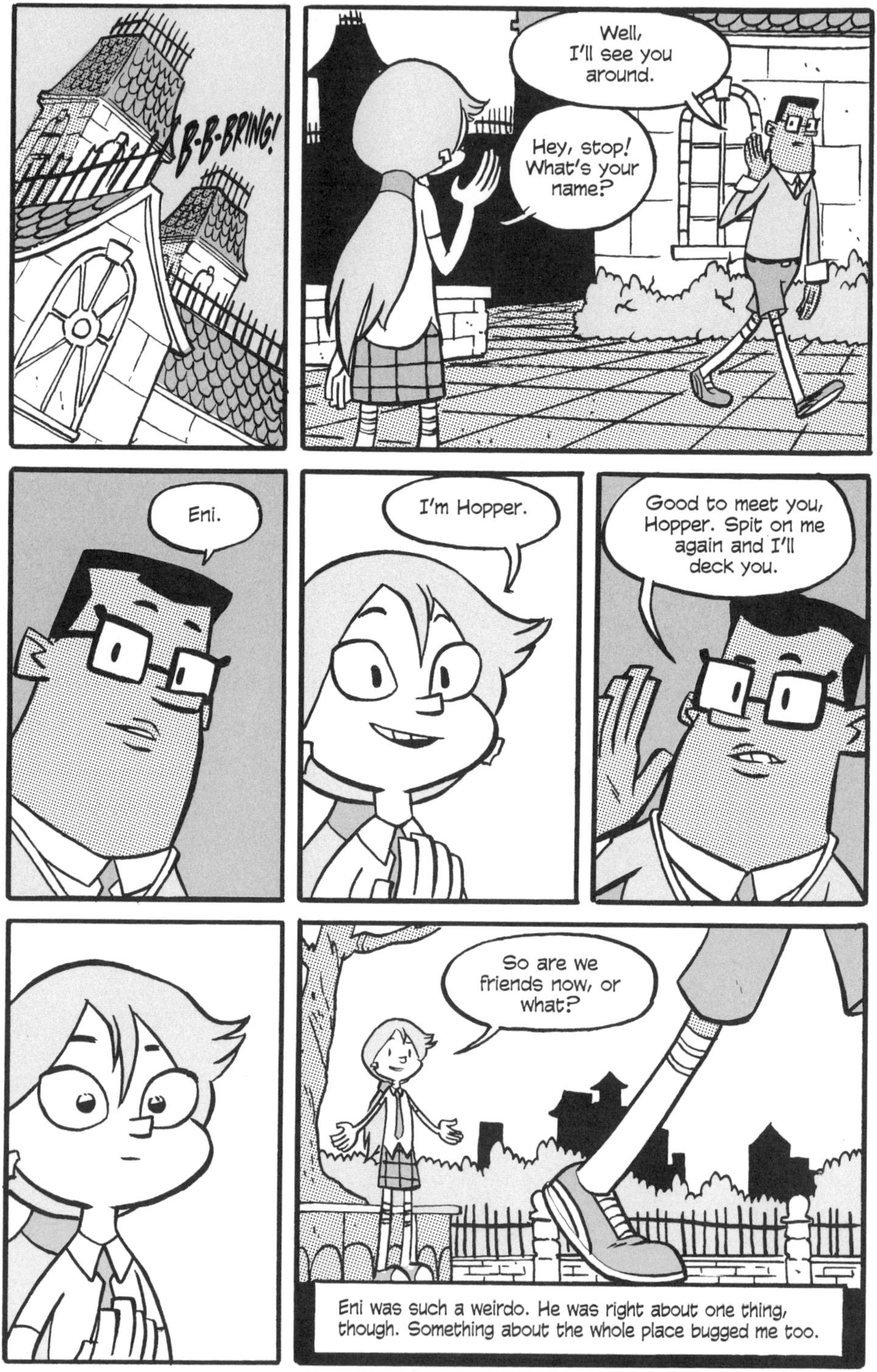
B-B-BRING!
Well, I'll see you around.
Hey, stop! What's your name?
Eni.
I'm Hopper.
Good to meet you, Hopper. Spit on me again and I'll deck you.
So are we friends now, or what?
Eni was such a weirdo. He was right about one thing, though. Something about the whole place bugged me too.

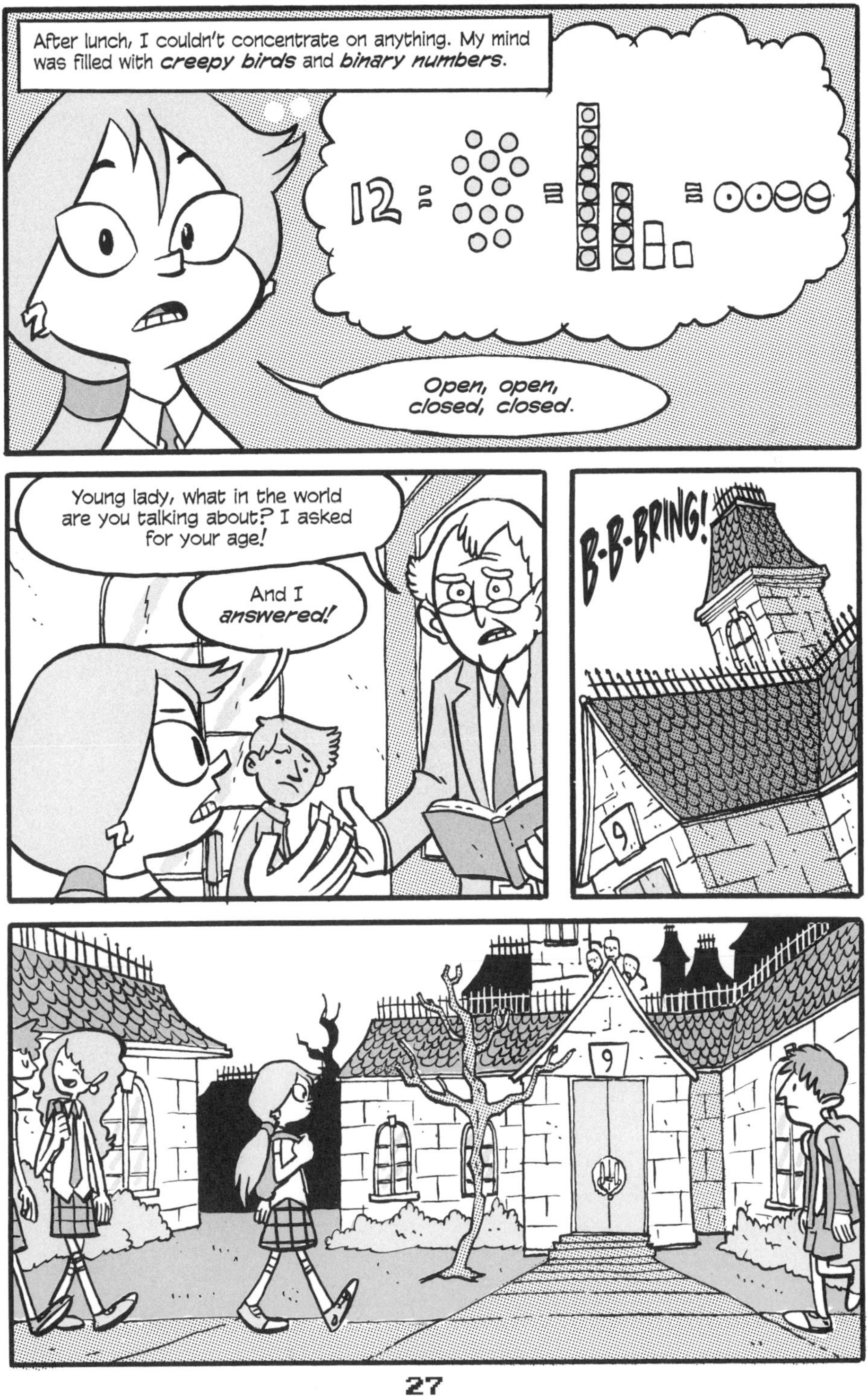
After lunch, I couldn't concentrate on anything. My mind was filled with ***creepy birds*** and ***binary numbers***.
12 = = = 0000
Open, open, closed, closed.
Young lady, what in the world are you talking about? I asked for your age!
And I *answered!*
B-B-BRING!
9
9

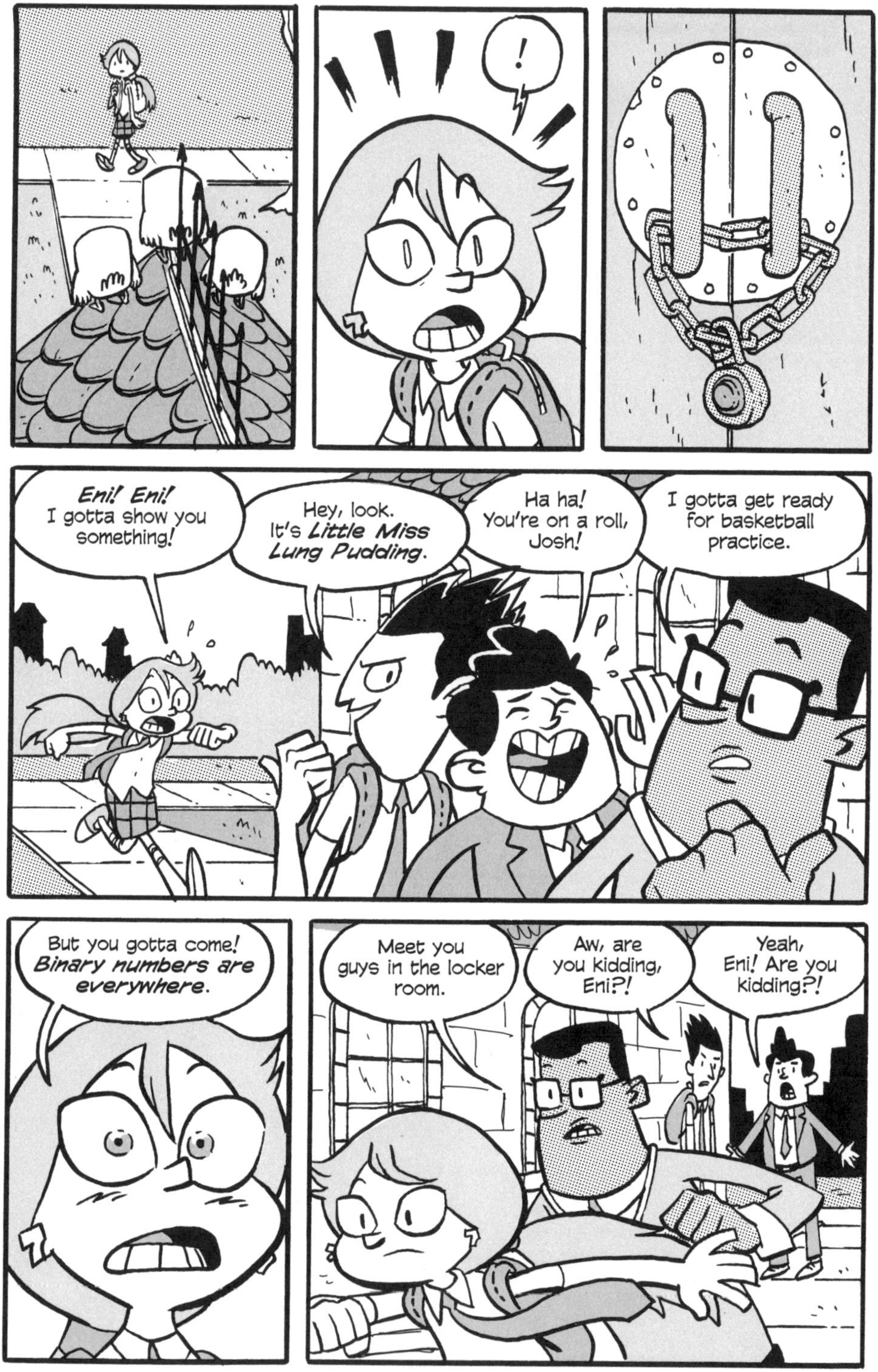
!
Eni! Eni! I gotta show you something!
Hey, look. It's Little Miss Lung Pudding.
Ha ha! You're on a roll, Josh!
I gotta get ready for basketball practice.
But you gotta come! Binary numbers are everywhere.
Meet you guys in the locker room.
Aw, are you kidding, Eni?!
Yeah, Eni! Are you kidding?!

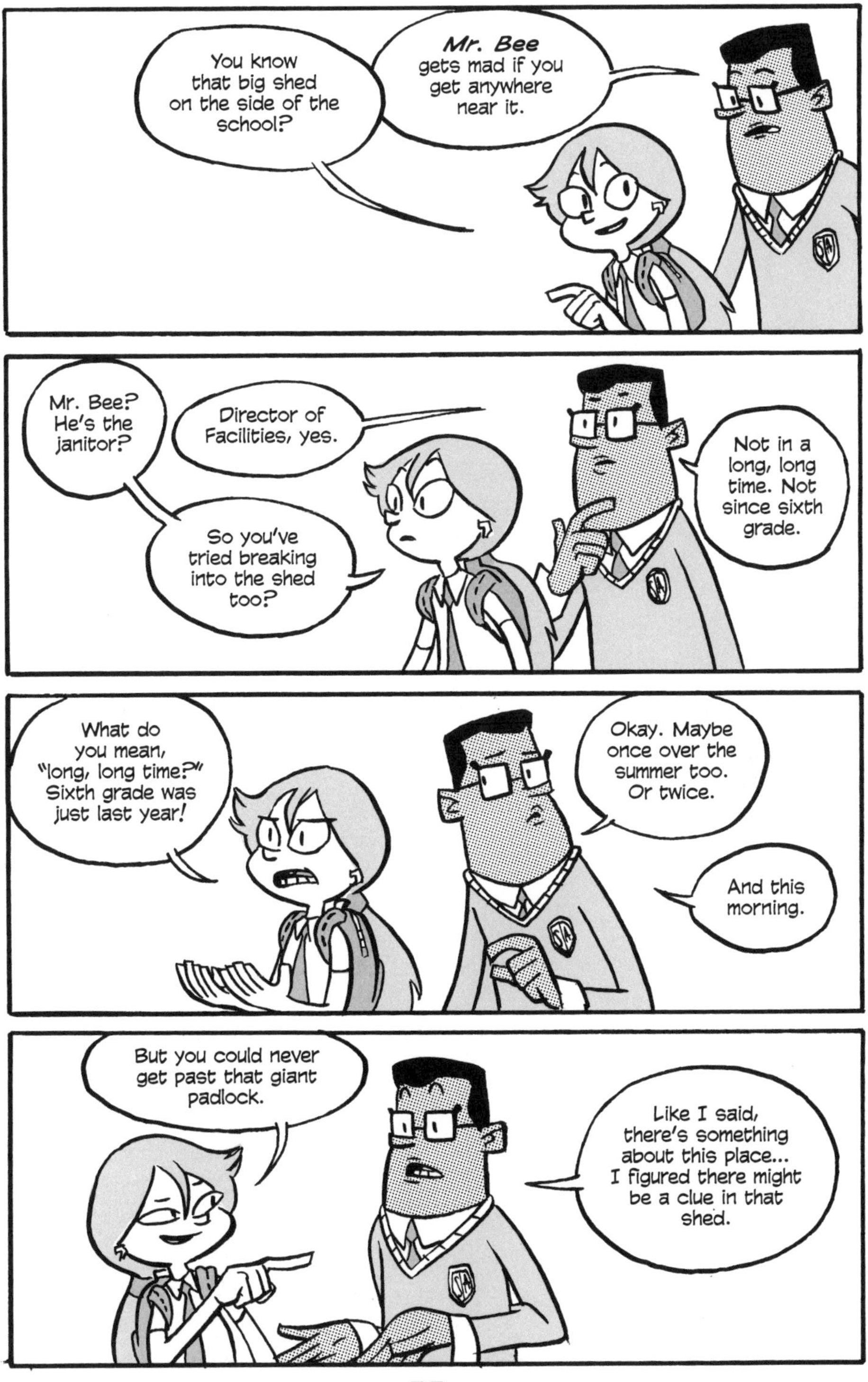
You know that big shed on the side of the school?
Mr. Bee gets mad if you get anywhere near it.
Mr. Bee? He's the janitor?
Director of Facilities, yes.
So you've tried breaking into the shed too?
Not in a long, long time. Not since sixth grade.
What do you mean, "long, long time?" Sixth grade was just last year!
Okay. Maybe once over the summer too. Or twice.
And this morning.
But you could never get past that giant padlock.
Like I said, there's something about this place... I figured there might be a clue in that shed.

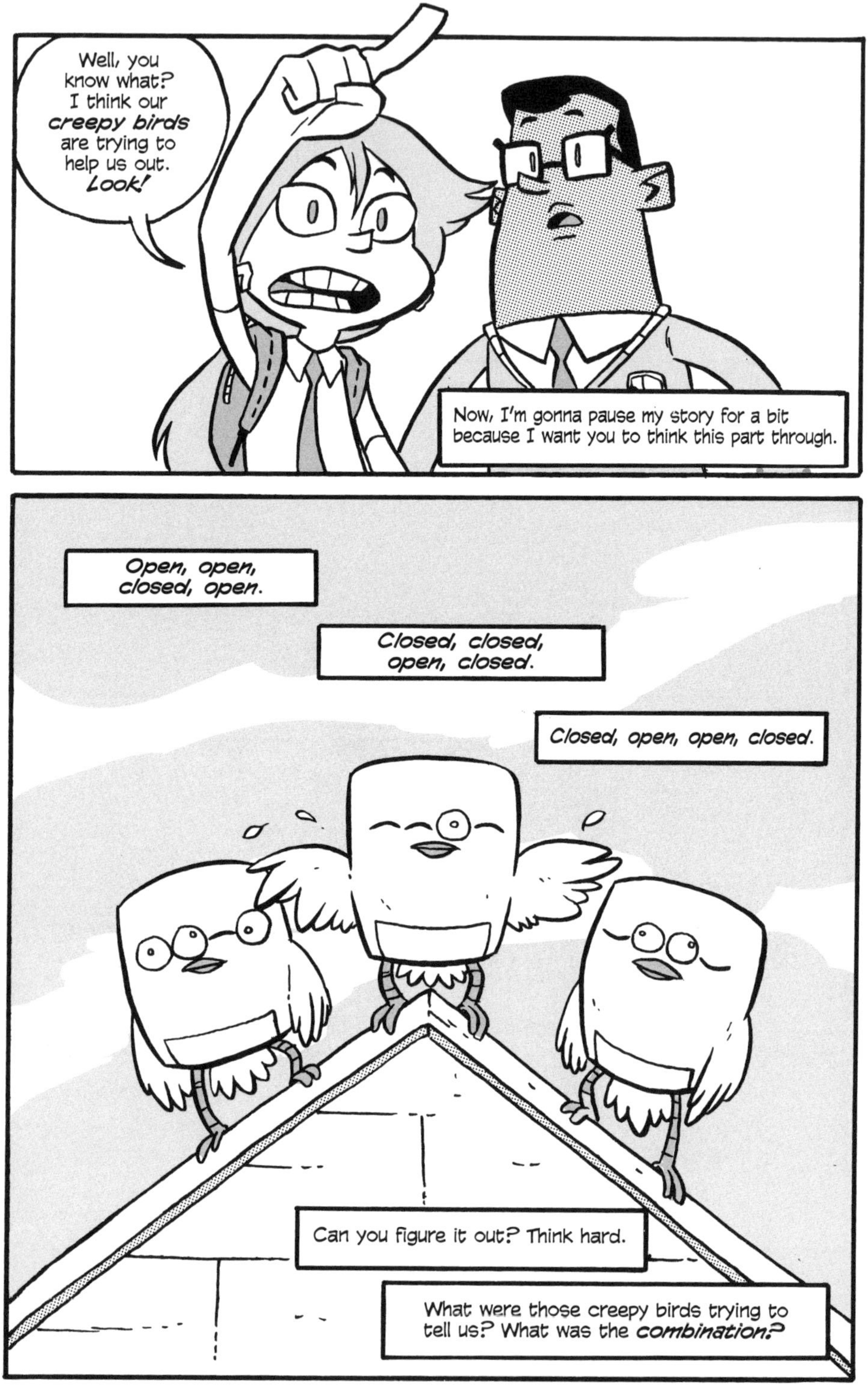
Well, you know what? I think our *creepy birds* are trying to help us out. *Look!*
Now, I'm gonna pause my story for a bit because I want you to think this part through.
Open, open, closed, open.
Closed, closed, open, closed.
Closed, open, open, closed.
Can you figure it out? Think hard.
What were those creepy birds trying to tell us? What was the *combination?*

Chapter

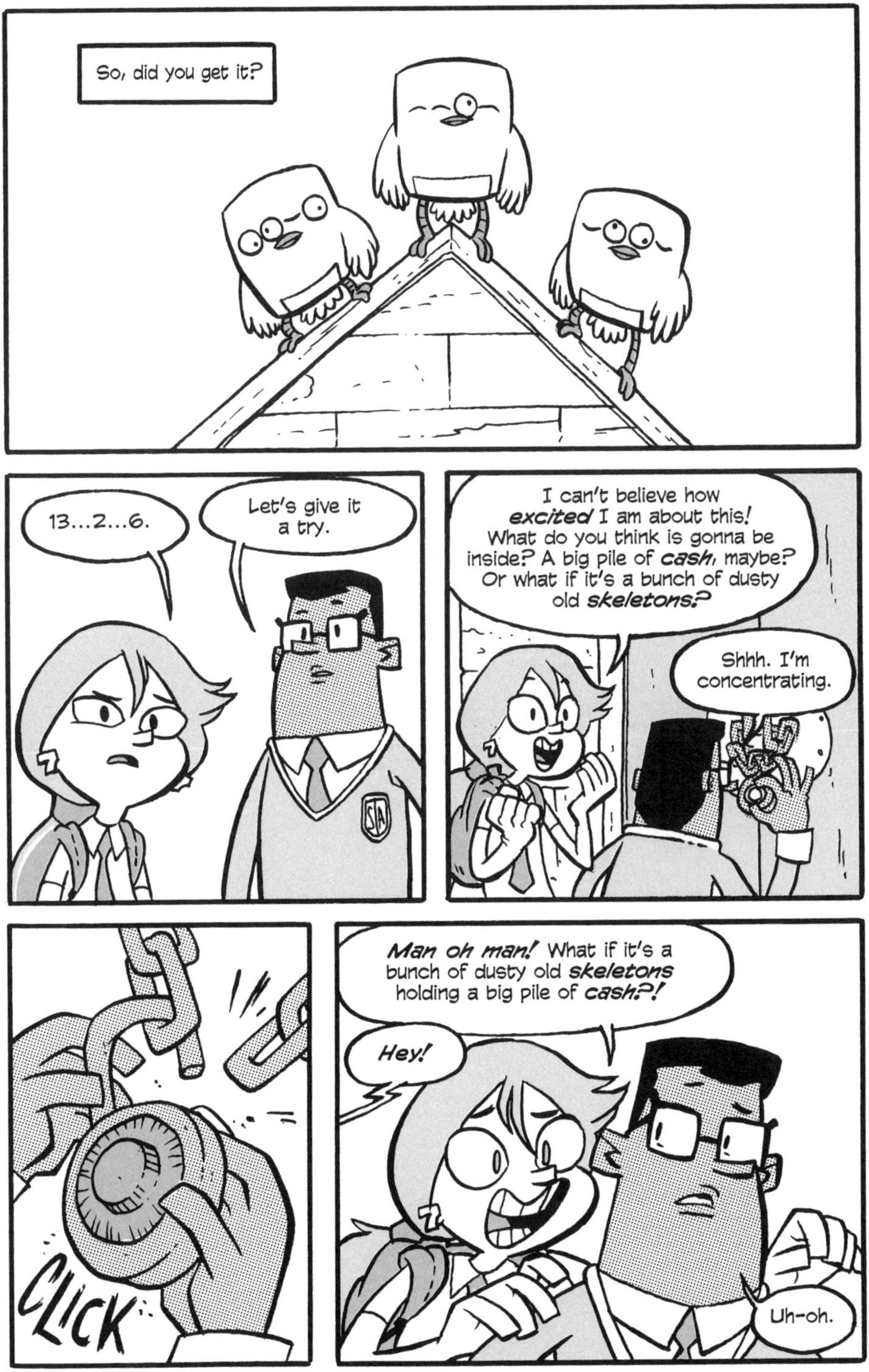

So, did you get it?
13...2...6.
Let's give it a try.
I can't believe how *excited* I am about this! What do you think is gonna be inside? A big pile of *cash*, maybe? Or what if it's a bunch of dusty old *skeletons?*
Shhh. I'm concentrating.
CLICK
Man oh man! What if it's a bunch of dusty old *skeletons* holding a big pile of *cash?!*
Hey!
Uh-oh.

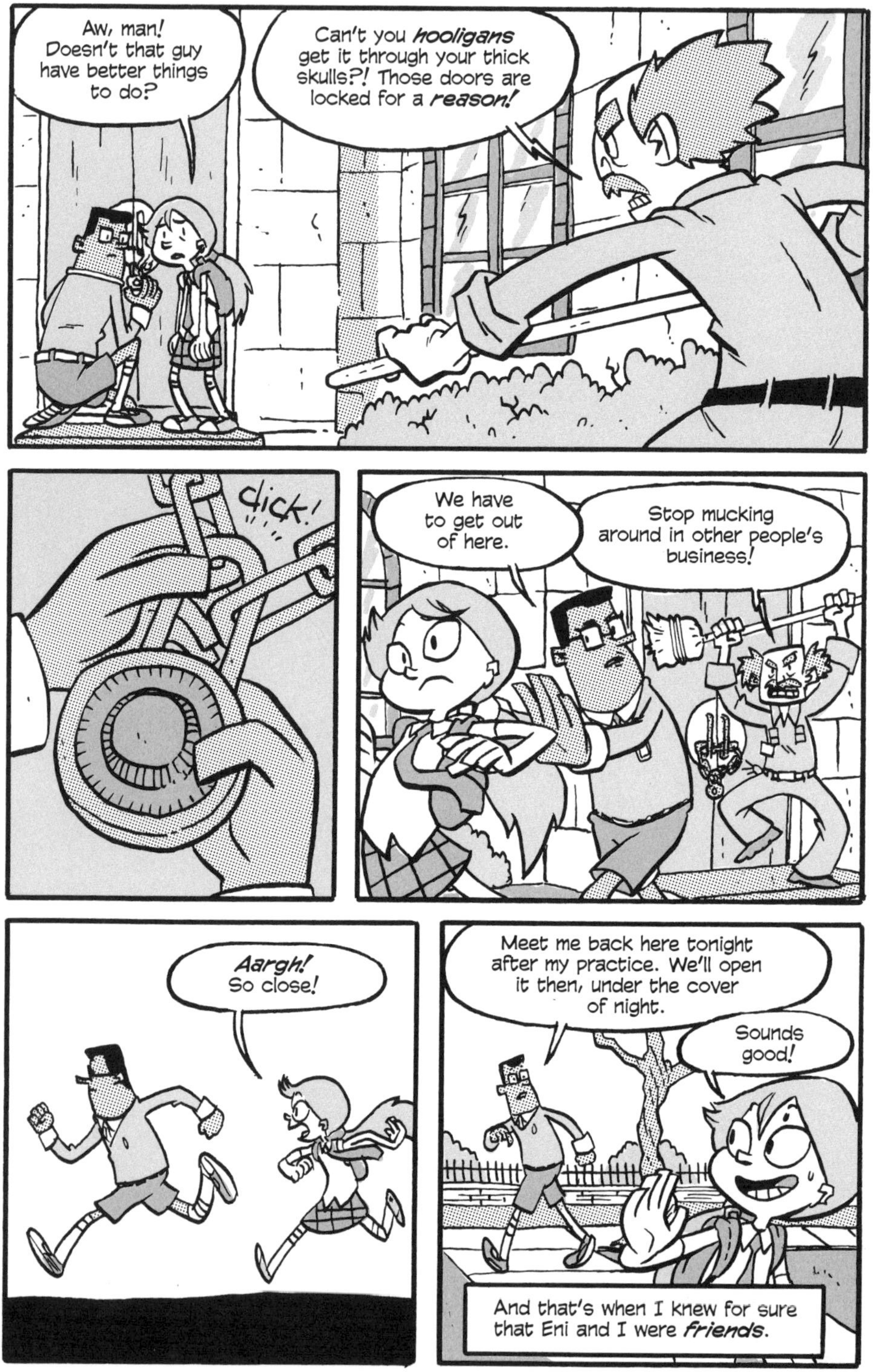

Aw, man! Doesn't that guy have better things to do?
Can't you *hooligans* get it through your thick skulls?! Those doors are locked for a *reason!*
Click!
We have to get out of here.
Stop mucking around in other people's business!
Aargh! So close!
Meet me back here tonight after my practice. We'll open it then, under the cover of night.
Sounds good!
And that's when I knew for sure that Eni and I were *friends*.

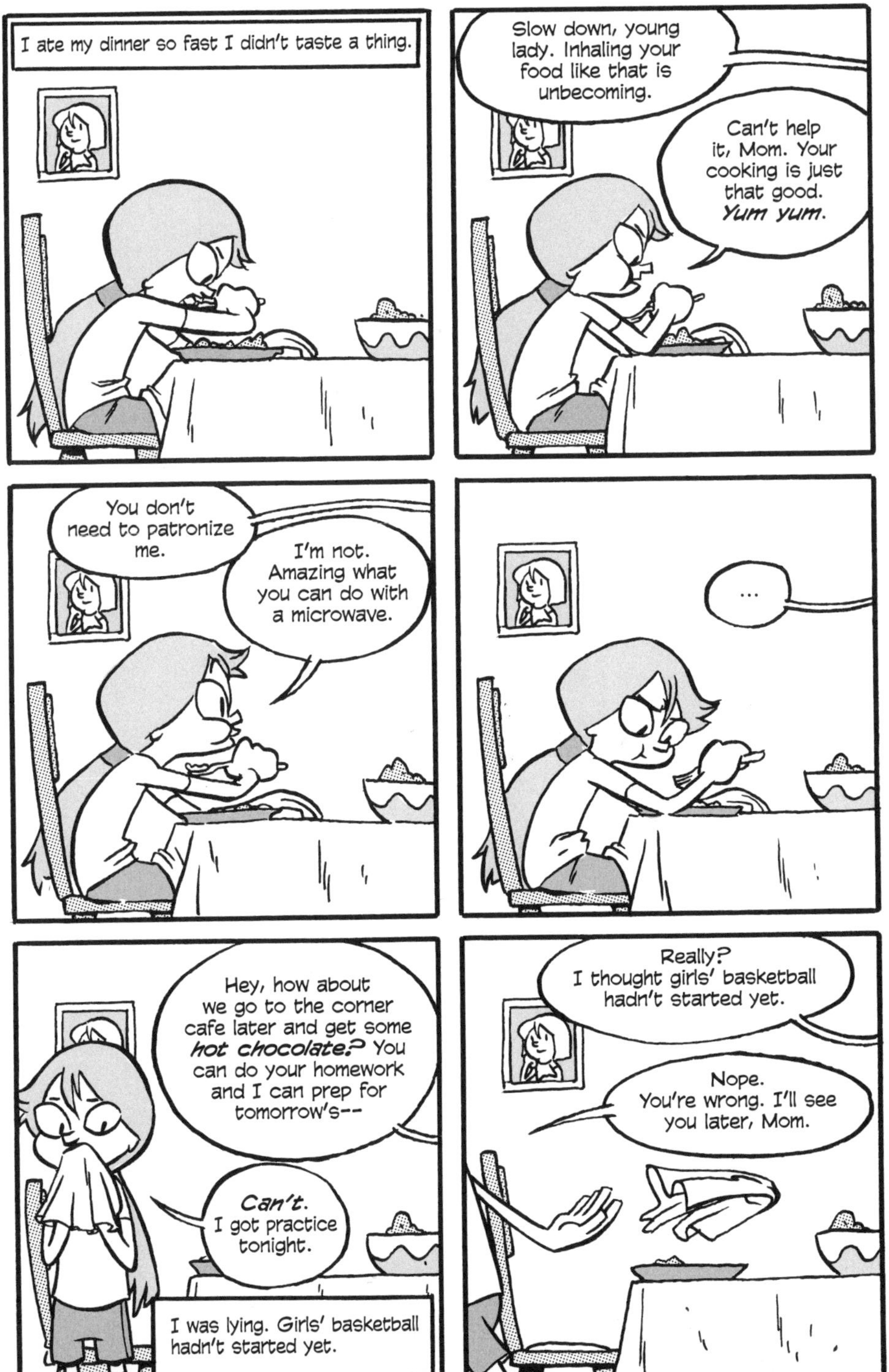

I ate my dinner so fast I didn't taste a thing.
Slow down, young lady. Inhaling your food like that is unbecoming.
Can't help it, Mom. Your cooking is just that good. *Yum yum.*
You don't need to patronize me.
I'm not. Amazing what you can do with a microwave.
...
Hey, how about we go to the corner cafe later and get some *hot chocolate?* You can do your homework and I can prep for tomorrow's--
Can't. I got practice tonight.
I was lying. Girls' basketball hadn't started yet.
Really? I thought girls' basketball hadn't started yet.
Nope. You're wrong. I'll see you later, Mom.

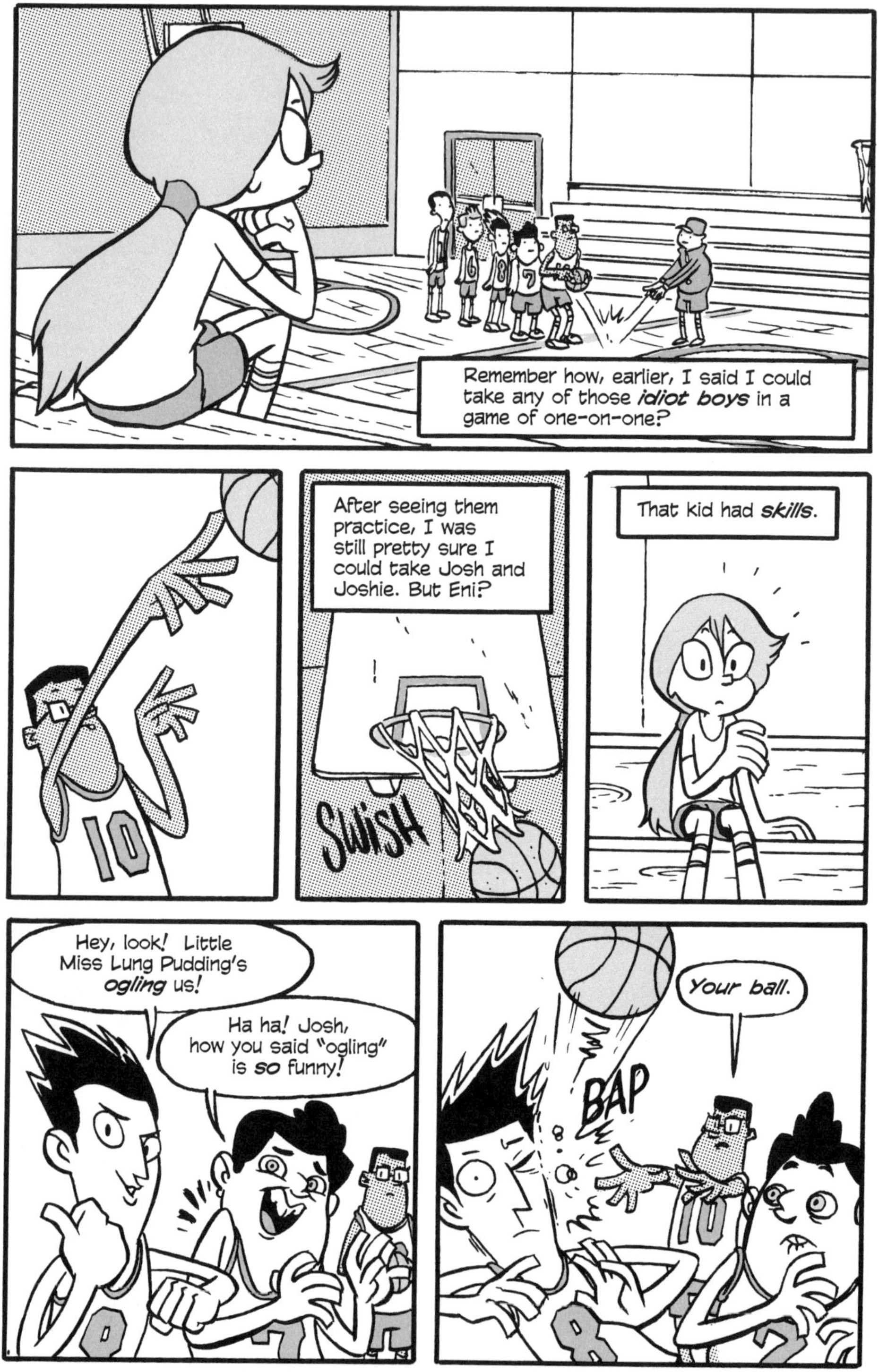
Remember how, earlier, I said I could take any of those *idiot boys* in a game of one-on-one?
After seeing them practice, I was still pretty sure I could take Josh and Joshie. But Eni?
SWISH
That kid had *skills*.
Hey, look! Little Miss Lung Pudding's *ogling* us!
Ha ha! Josh, how you said "ogling" is *so* funny!
Your ball.
BAP

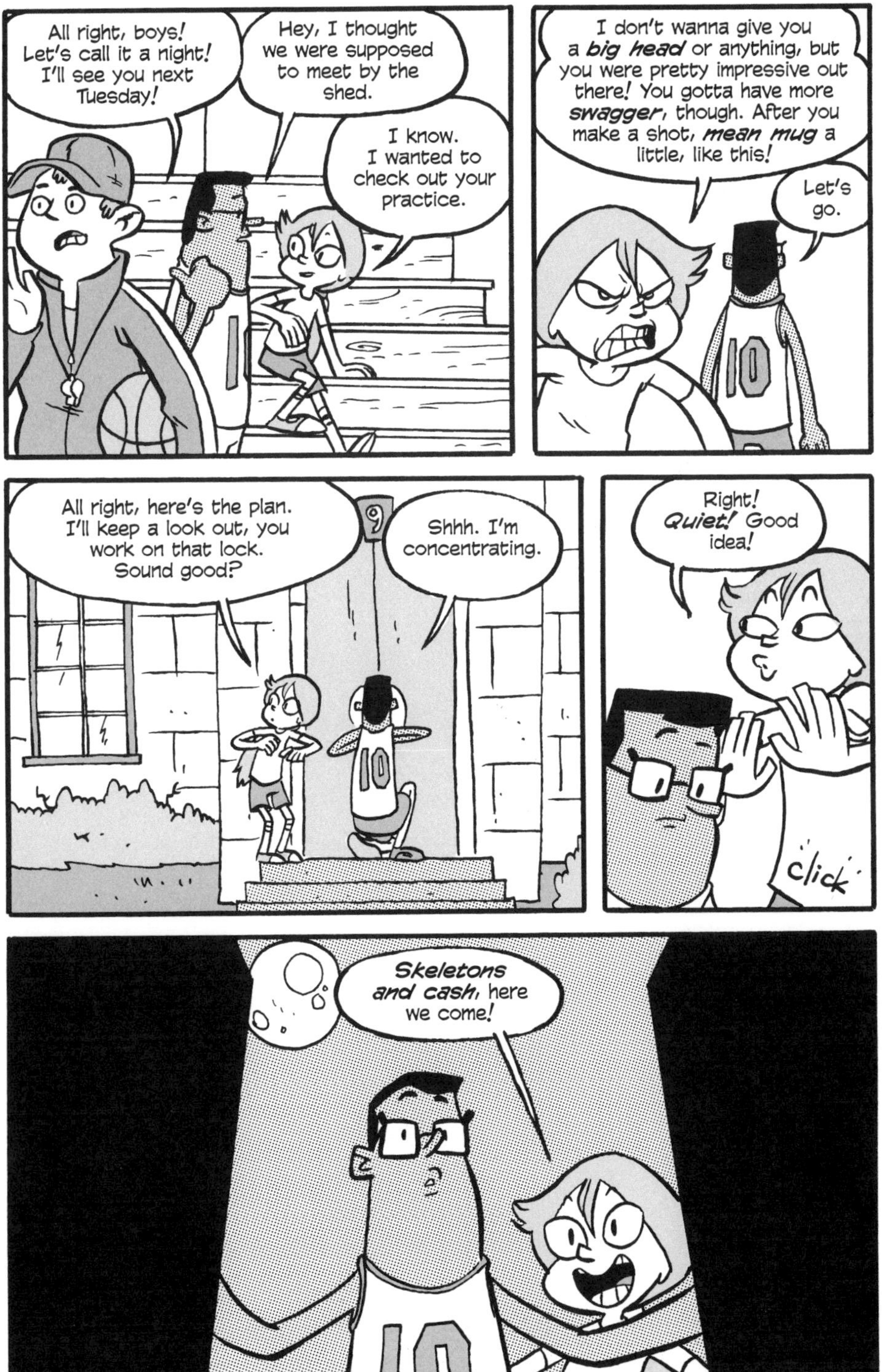
All right, boys! Let's call it a night! I'll see you next Tuesday!
Hey, I thought we were supposed to meet by the shed.
I know. I wanted to check out your practice.
I don't wanna give you a ***big head*** or anything, but you were pretty impressive out there! You gotta have more ***swagger***, though. After you make a shot, ***mean mug*** a little, like this!
Let's go.
All right, here's the plan. I'll keep a look out, you work on that lock. Sound good?
9
Shhh. I'm concentrating.
Right! ***Quiet!*** Good idea!
click
Skeletons and cash, here we come!
10

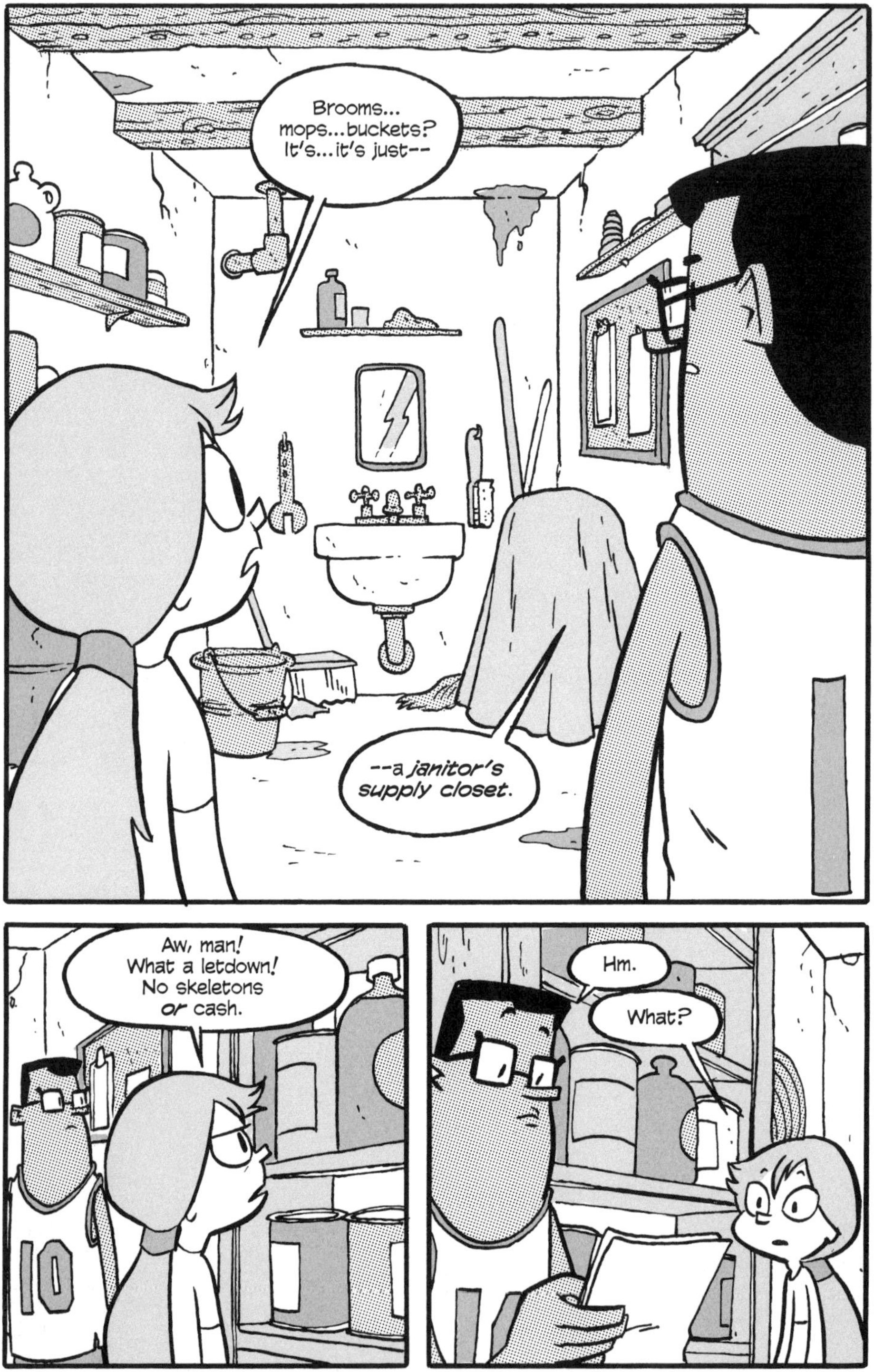
Brooms... mops...buckets? It's...it's just--
--a janitor's supply closet.
Aw, man! What a letdown! No skeletons or cash.
10
Hm.
What?

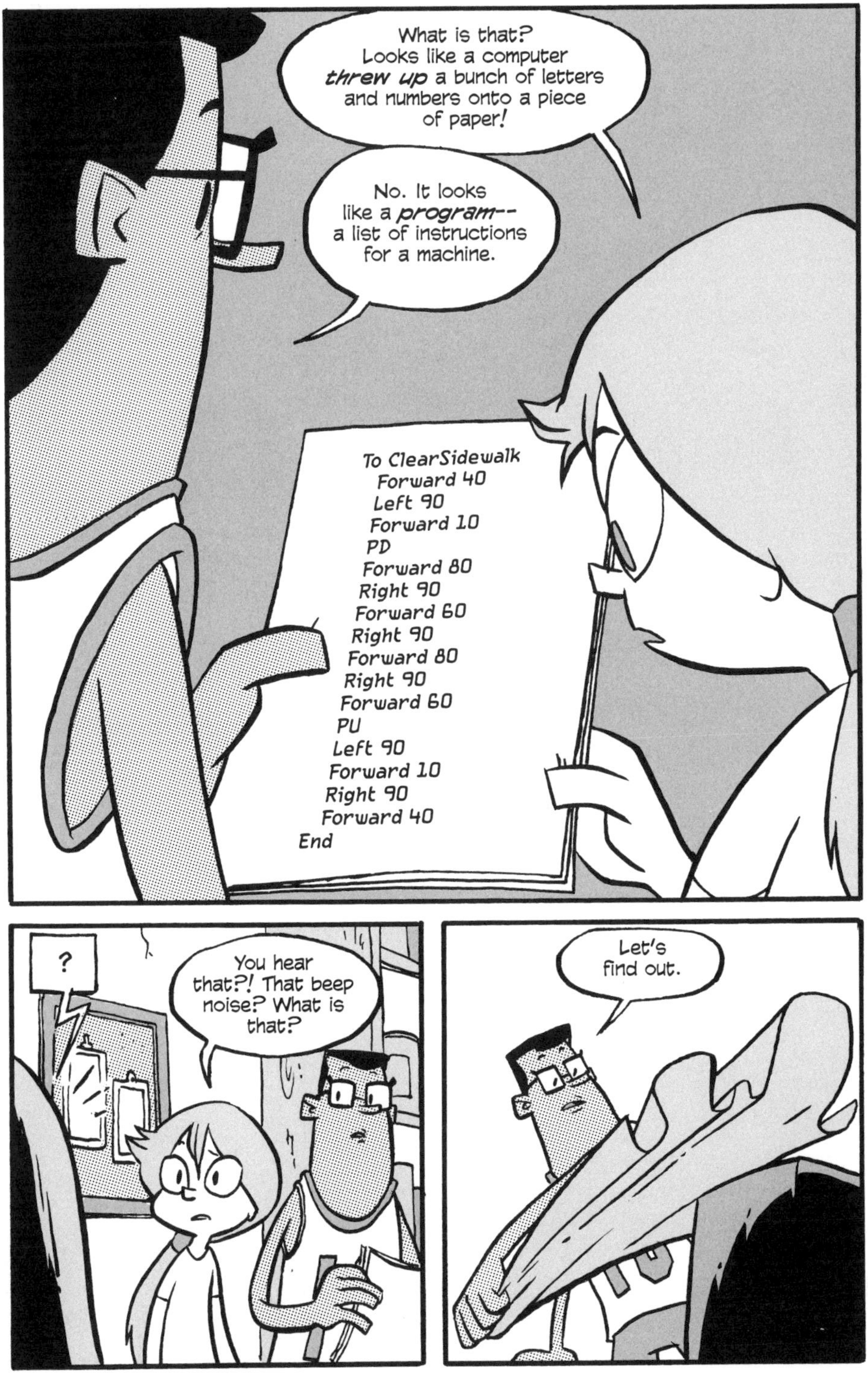
What is that? Looks like a computer *threw up* a bunch of letters and numbers onto a piece of paper!
No. It looks like a *program*-- a list of instructions for a machine.
To ClearSidewalk
Forward 40
Left 90
Forward 10
PD
Forward 80
Right 90
Forward 60
Right 90
Forward 80
Right 90
Forward 60
PU
Left 90
Forward 10
Right 90
Forward 40
End
?
You hear that?! That beep noise? What is that?
Let's find out.

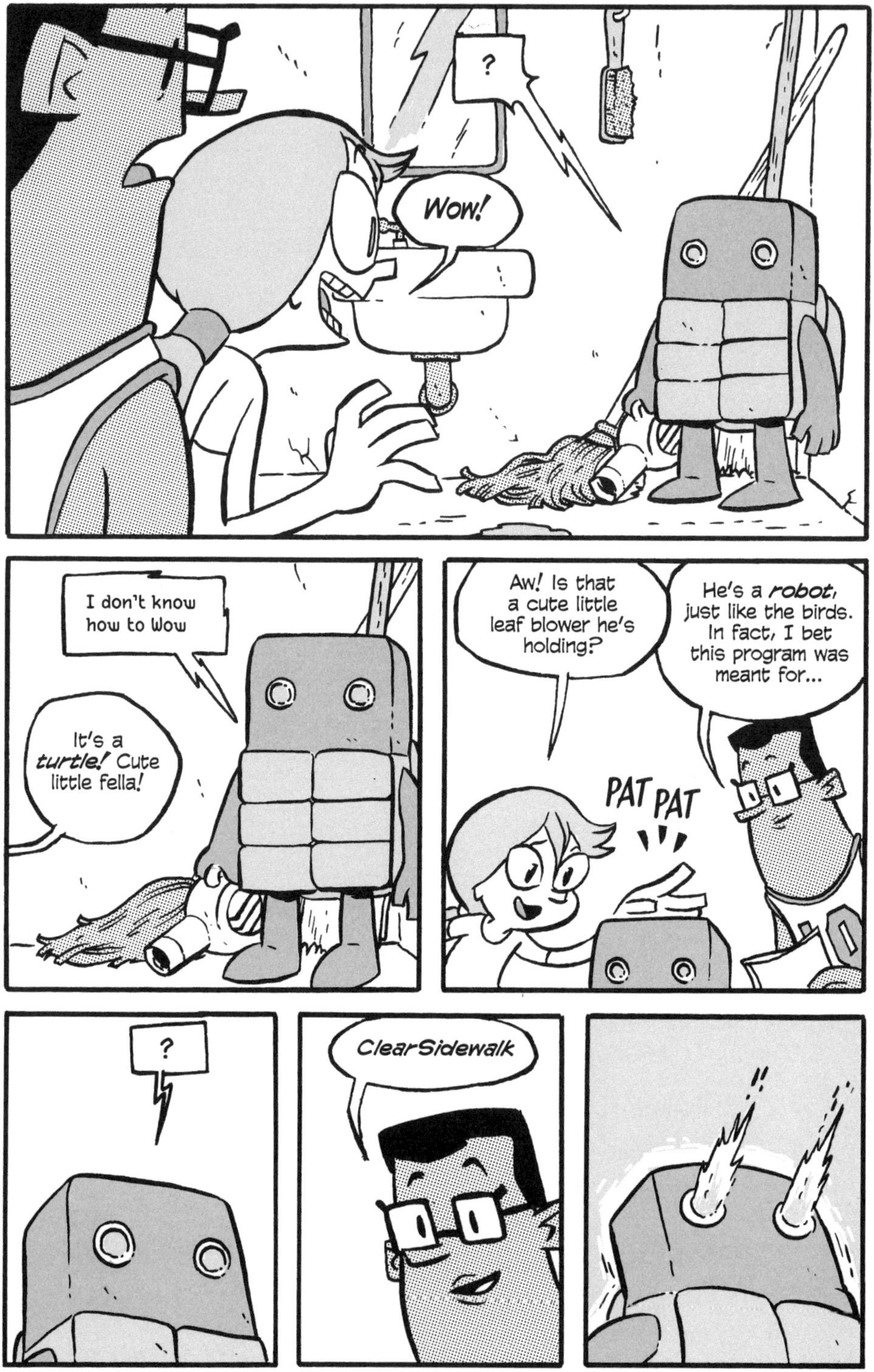
?
Wow!
I don't know how to Wow
It's a *turtle!* Cute little fella!
Aw! Is that a cute little leaf blower he's holding?
He's a *robot,* just like the birds. In fact, I bet this program was meant for...
PAT PAT
?
ClearSidewalk

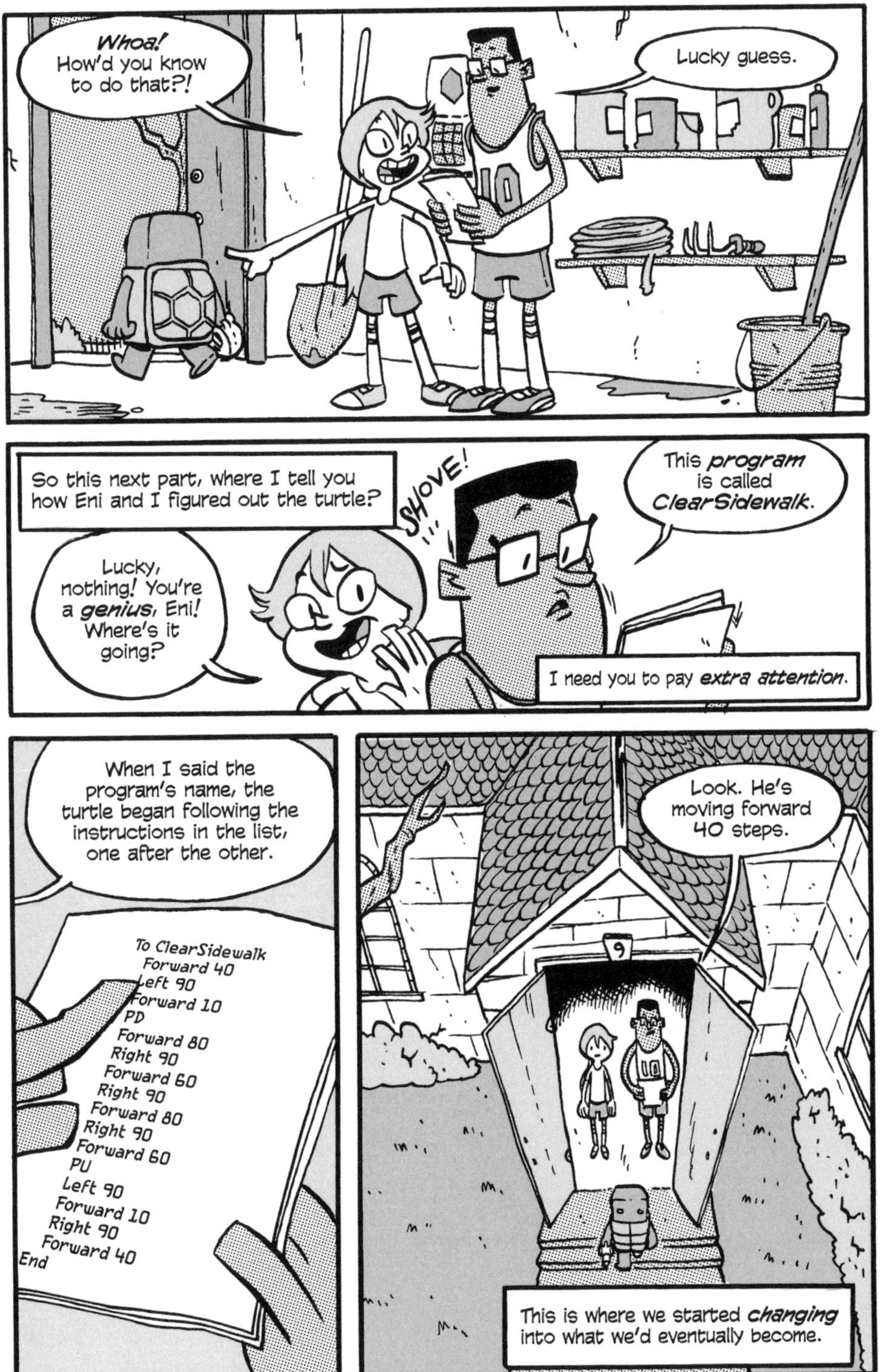
Whoa! How'd you know to do that?!
Lucky guess.
So this next part, where I tell you how Eni and I figured out the turtle?
SHOVE!
This program is called ClearSidewalk.
Lucky, nothing! You're a genius, Eni! Where's it going?
I need you to pay extra attention.
When I said the program's name, the turtle began following the instructions in the list, one after the other.
To ClearSidewalk
Forward 40
Left 90
Forward 10
PD
Forward 80
Right 90
Forward 60
Right 90
Forward 80
Right 90
Forward 60
PU
Left 90
Forward 10
Right 90
Forward 40
End
Look. He's moving forward 40 steps.
9
10
This is where we started changing into what we'd eventually become.

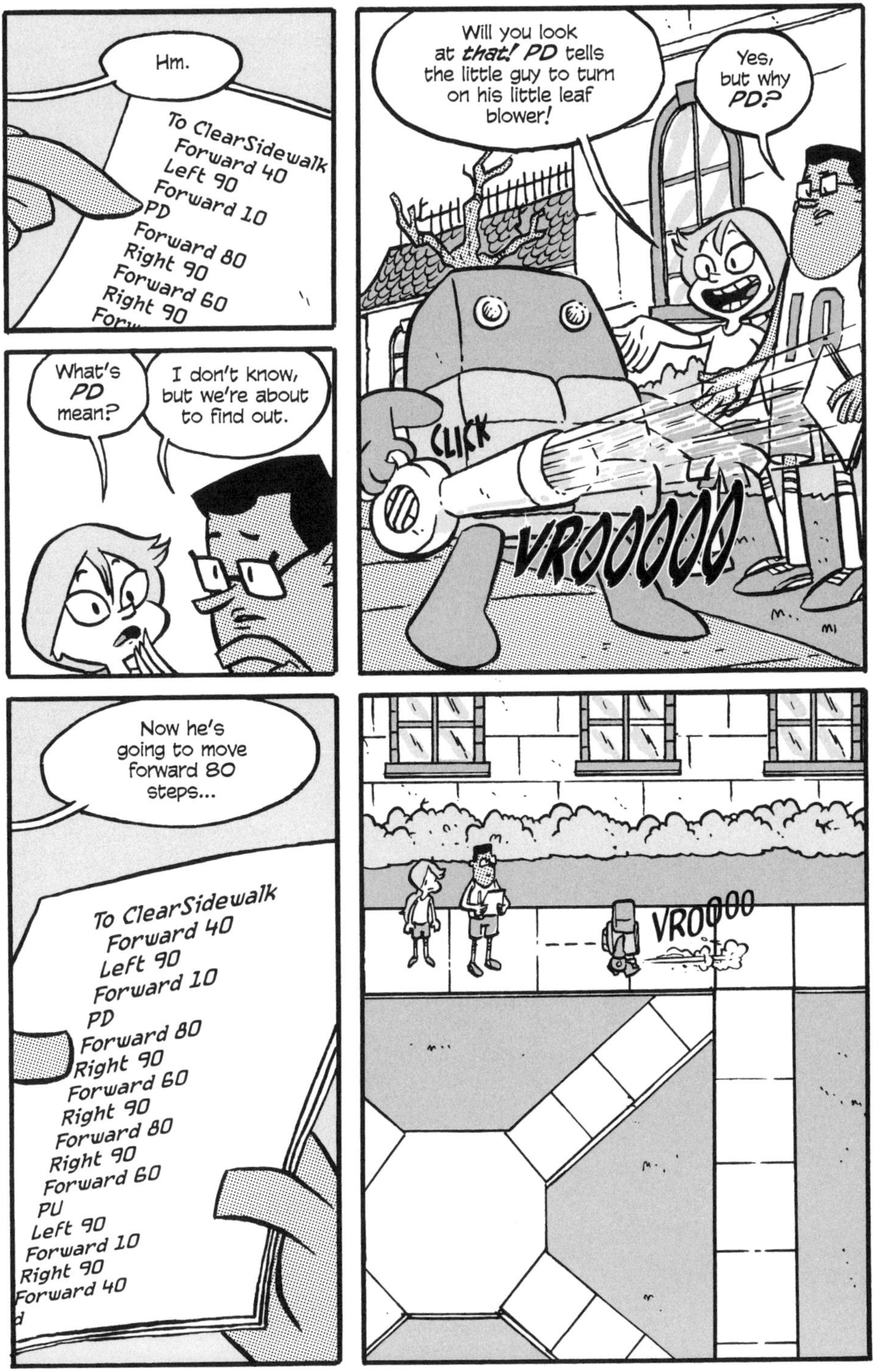
Hm.
To ClearSidewalk
Forward 40
Left 90
Forward 10
PD
Forward 80
Right 90
Forward 60
Right 90
Will you look at that! PD tells the little guy to turn on his little leaf blower!
Yes, but why PD?
CLICK
VROOOOO
What's PD mean?
I don't know, but we're about to find out.
Now he's going to move forward 80 steps...
To ClearSidewalk
Forward 40
Left 90
Forward 10
PD
Forward 80
Right 90
Forward 60
Right 90
Forward 80
Right 90
Forward 60
PU
Left 90
Forward 10
Right 90
Forward 40
VROOOO

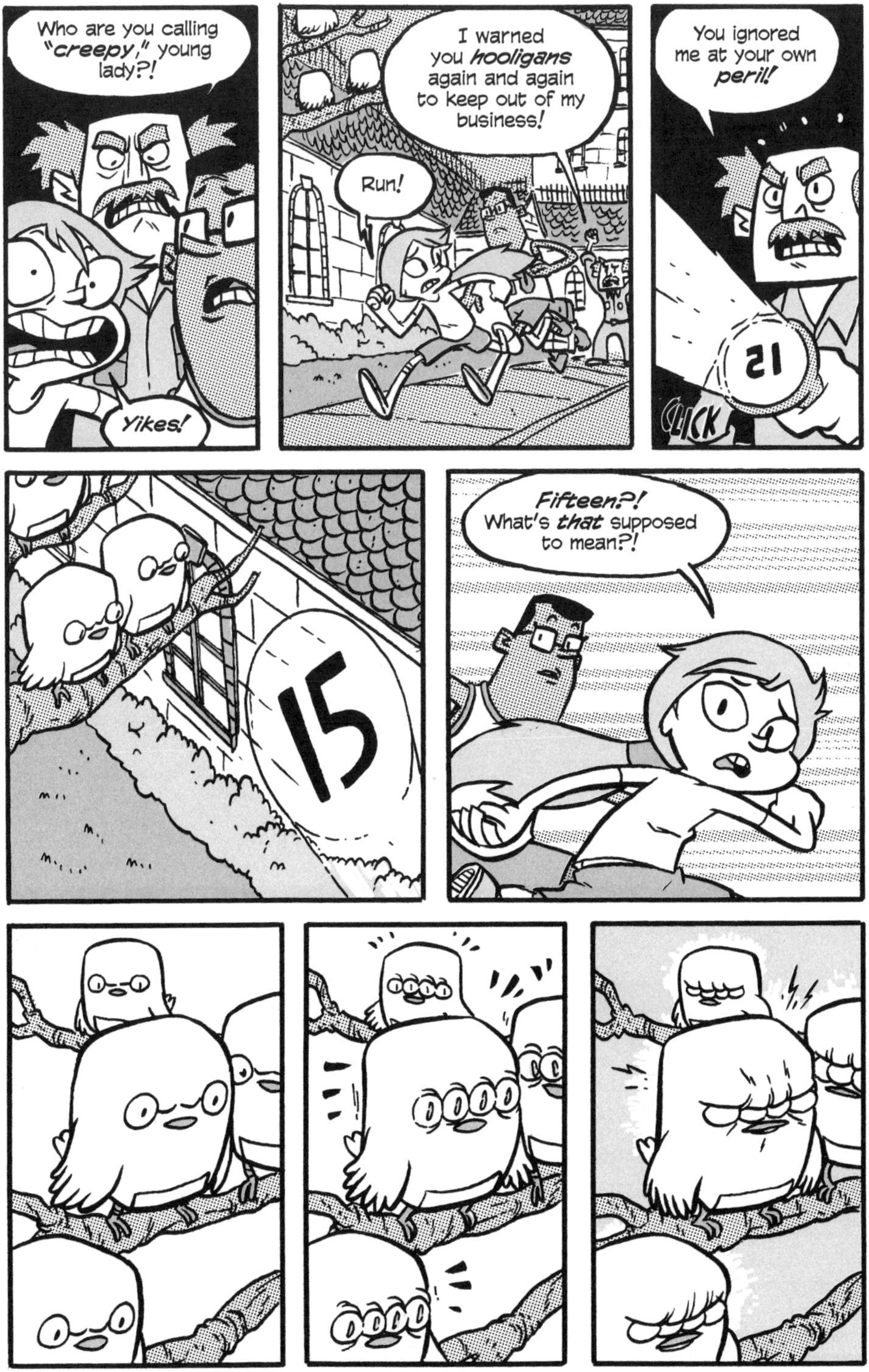
Who are you calling "creepy," young lady?!
Yikes!
I warned you hooligans again and again to keep out of my business!
Run!
You ignored me at your own peril!
21
CLICK
15
Fifteen?! What's that supposed to mean?!

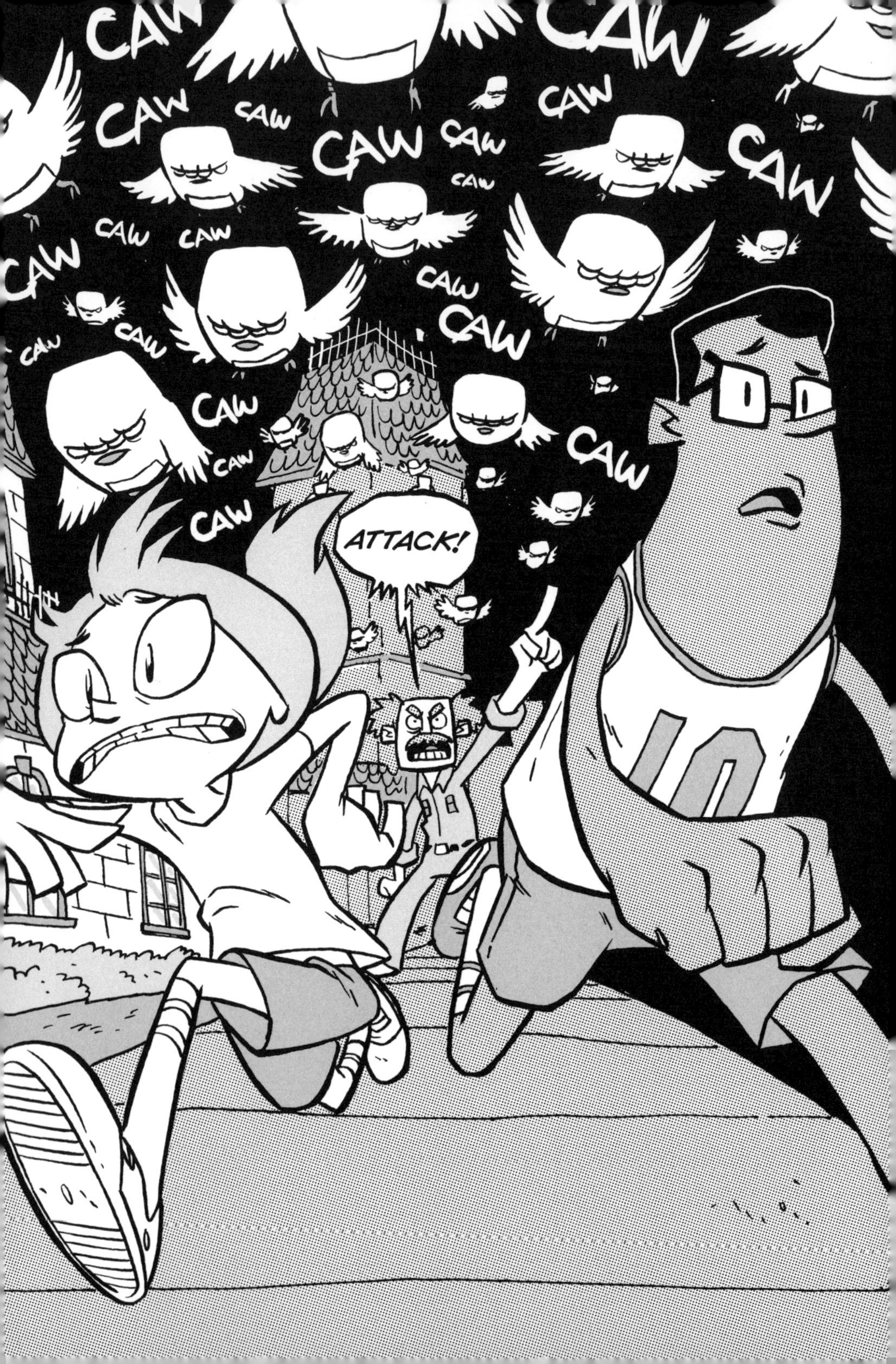
CAW
CAW
CAW
CAW
CAW
CAW
CAW
CAW
CAW
CAW
CAW
CAW
CAW
CAW
CAW
CAW
CAW
CAW
CAW
CAW
ATTACK!

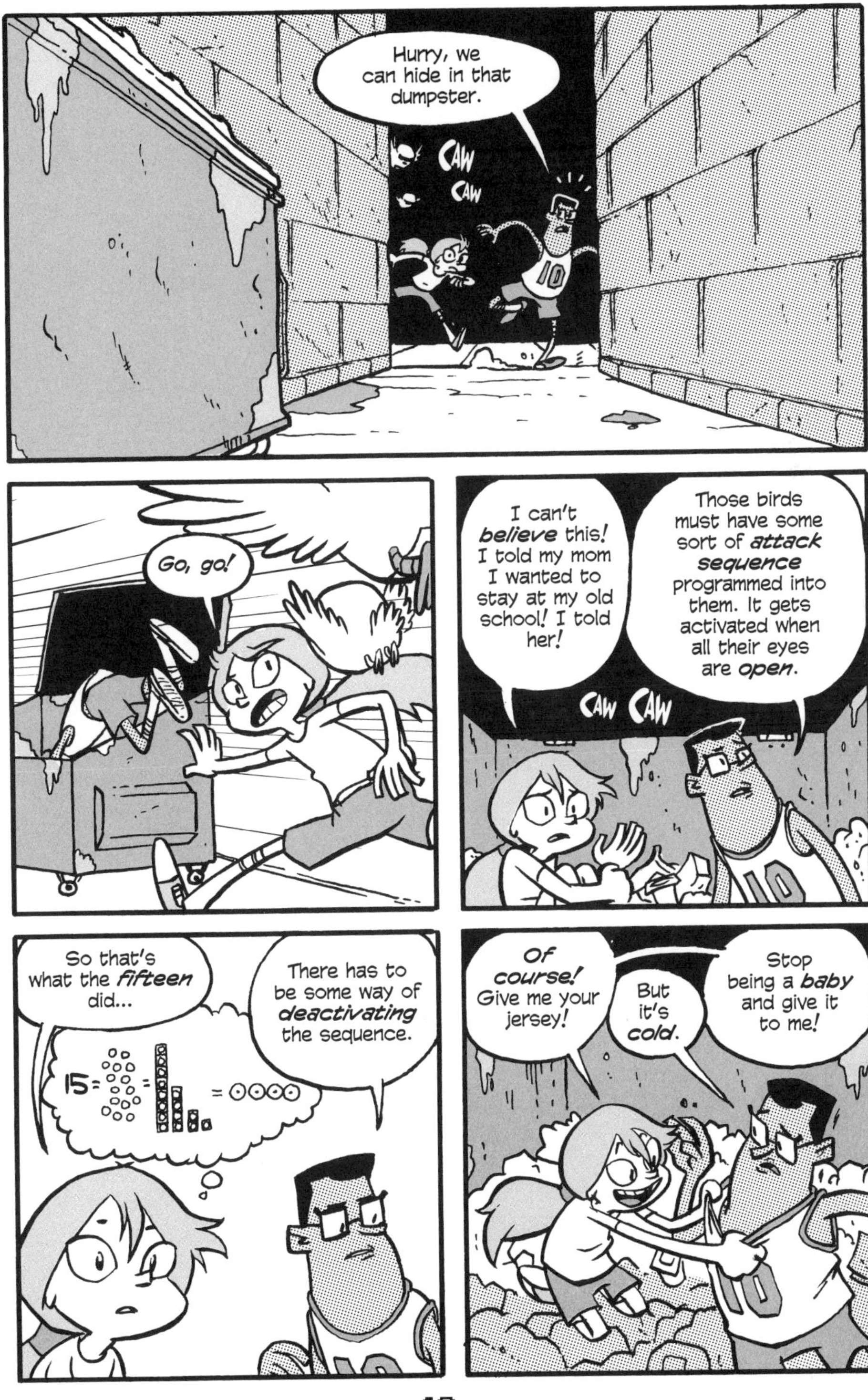
Hurry, we can hide in that dumpster.
CAW
CAW
Go, go!
I can't *believe* this! I told my mom I wanted to stay at my old school! I told her!
Those birds must have some sort of *attack sequence* programmed into them. It gets activated when all their eyes are *open*.
CAW CAW
So that's what the *fifteen* did...
15 = = = OOOO
There has to be some way of *deactivating* the sequence.
Of course! Give me your jersey!
But it's *cold*.
Stop being a *baby* and give it to me!

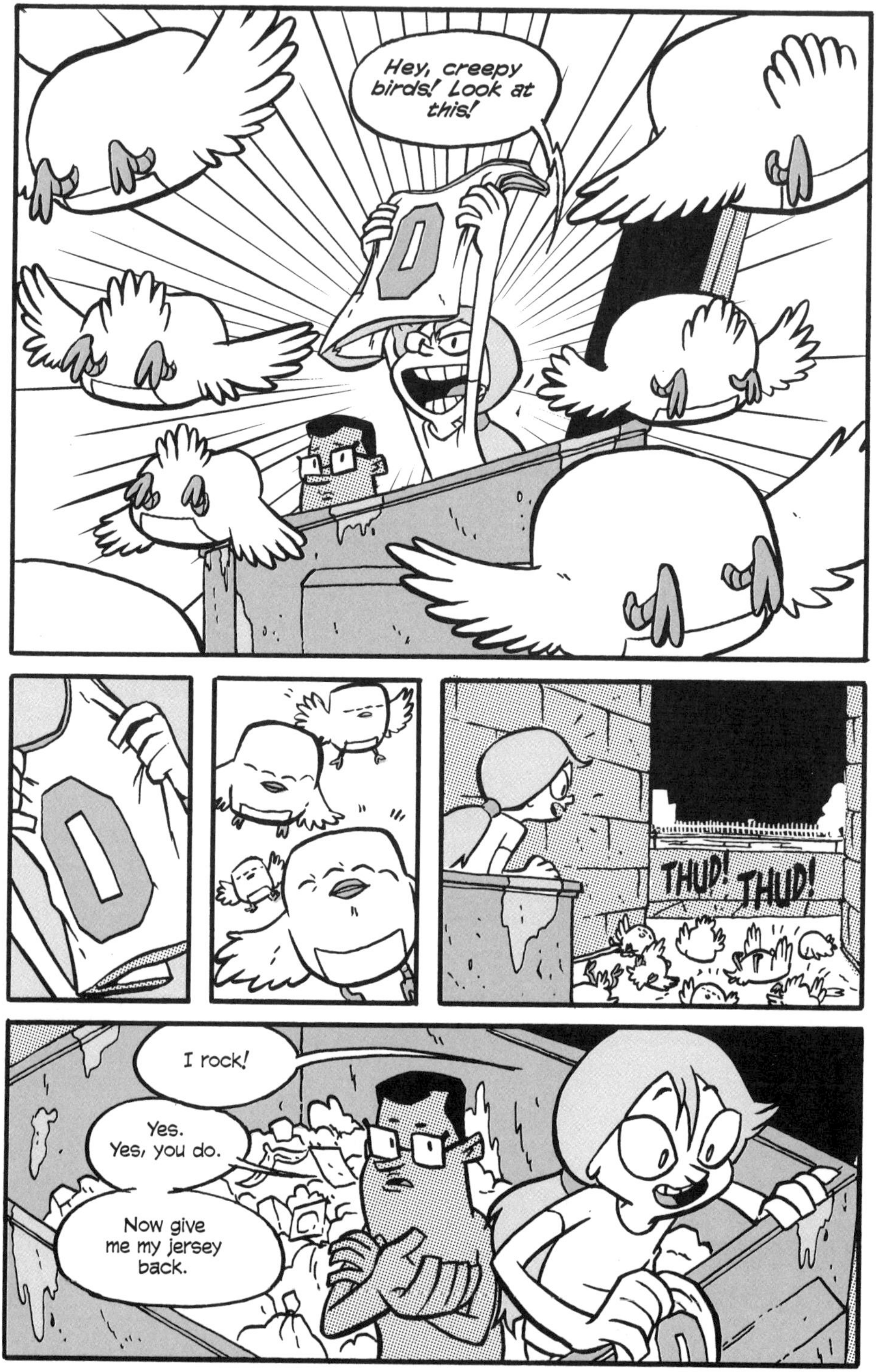
Hey, creepy birds! Look at this!
THUD! THUD!
I rock!
Yes. Yes, you do.
Now give me my jersey back.

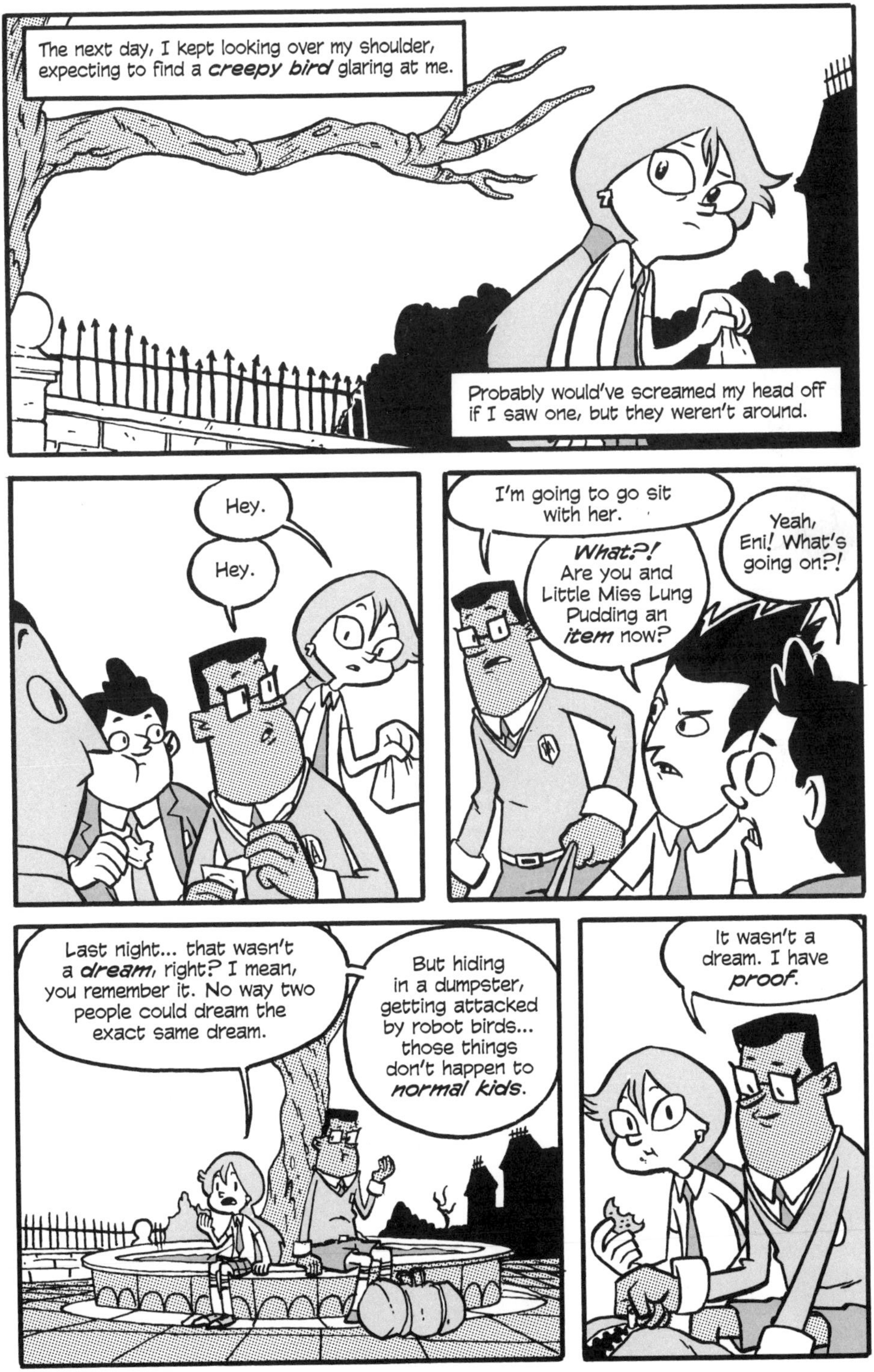
The next day, I kept looking over my shoulder, expecting to find a *creepy bird* glaring at me.
Probably would've screamed my head off if I saw one, but they weren't around.
Hey.
Hey.
I'm going to go sit with her.
What?! Are you and Little Miss Lung Pudding an *item* now?
Yeah, Eni! What's going on?!
Last night... that wasn't a *dream*, right? I mean, you remember it. No way two people could dream the exact same dream.
But hiding in a dumpster, getting attacked by robot birds... those things don't happen to *normal kids*.
It wasn't a dream. I have *proof*.

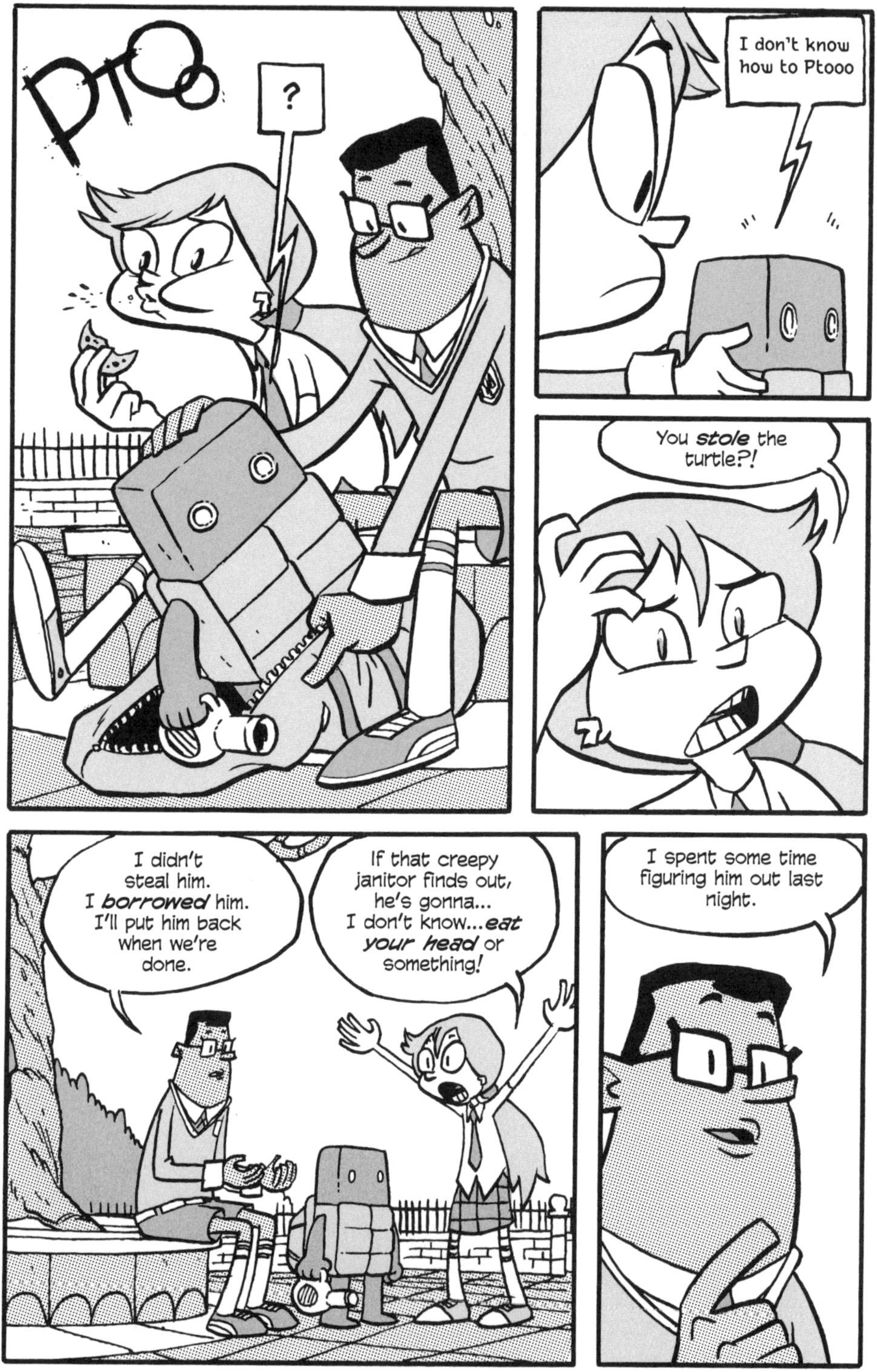
PTOOO
?
I don't know how to Ptooo
You *stole* the turtle?!
I didn't steal him. I *borrowed* him. I'll put him back when we're done.
If that creepy janitor finds out, he's gonna... I don't know...*eat your head* or something!
I spent some time figuring him out last night.

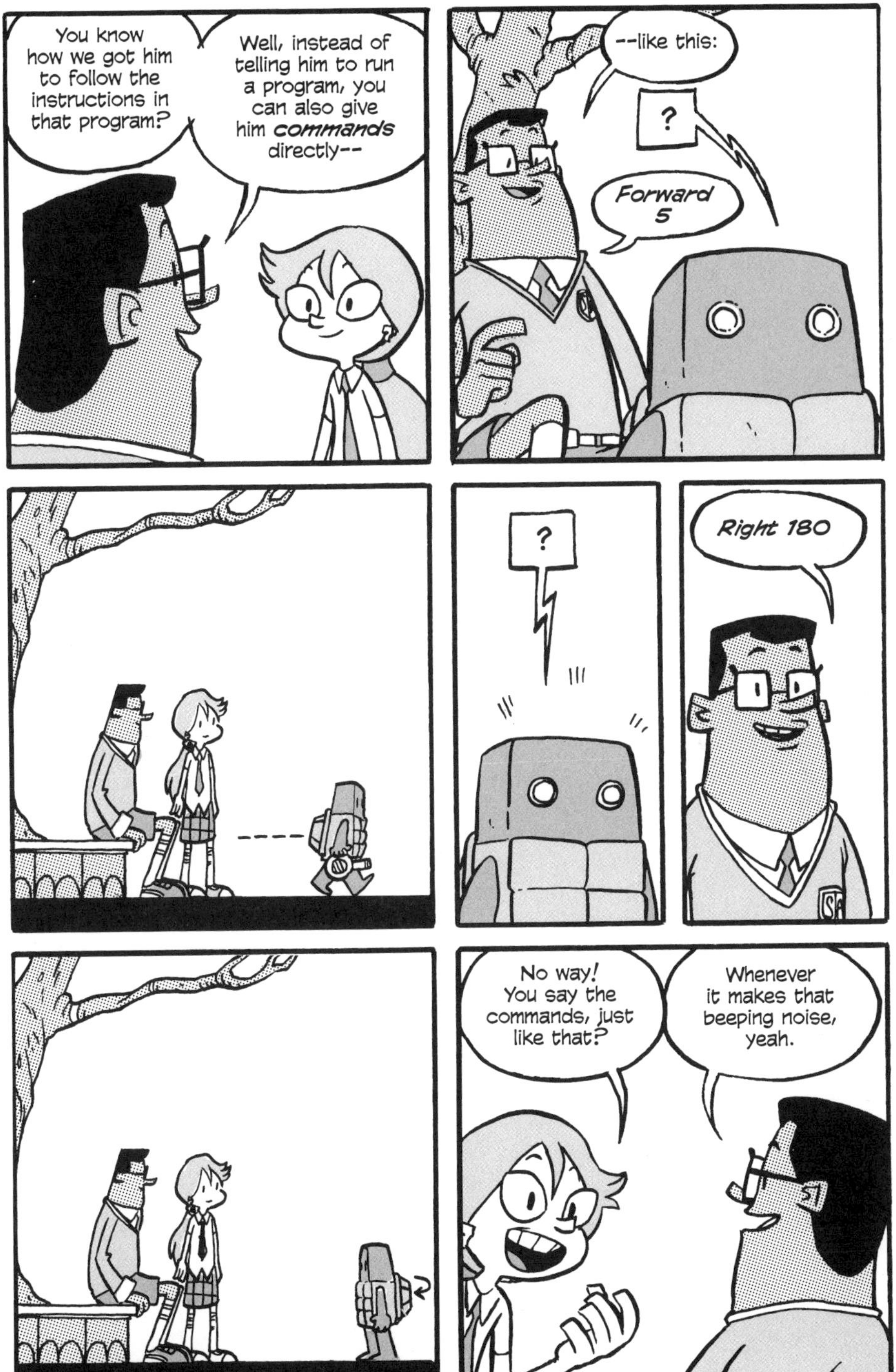
You know how we got him to follow the instructions in that program?
Well, instead of telling him to run a program, you can also give him ***commands*** directly--
--like this:
?
Forward 5
?
Right 180
No way! You say the commands, just like that?
Whenever it makes that beeping noise, yeah.

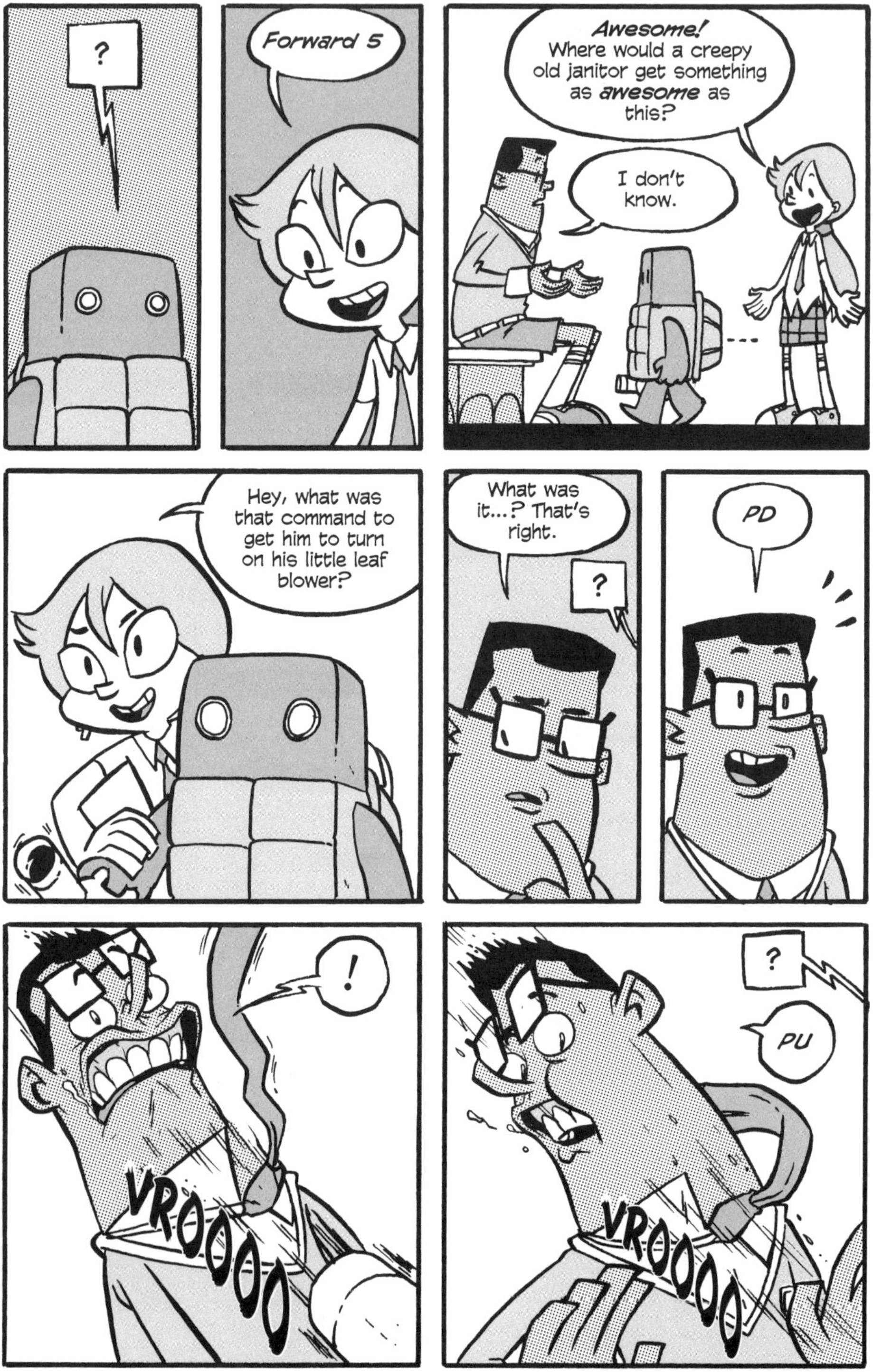
?
Forward 5
Awesome! Where would a creepy old janitor get something as **awesome** as this?
I don't know.
Hey, what was that command to get him to turn on his little leaf blower?
What was it...? That's right.
?
PD
!
VROOOOO
?
PU
VROOOOO

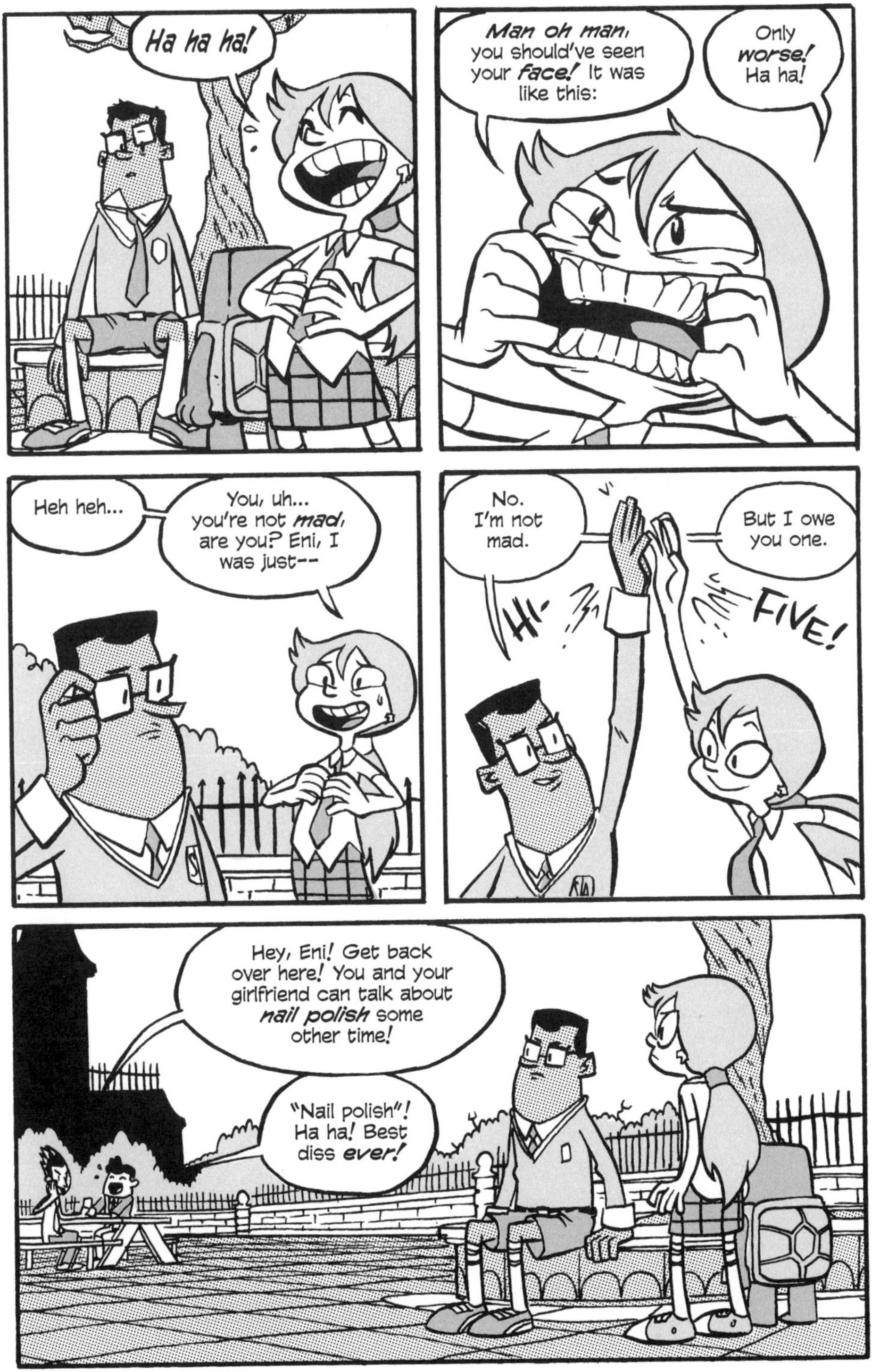
Ha ha ha!
Man oh man, you should've seen your face! It was like this:
Only worse! Ha ha!
Heh heh...
You, uh... you're not mad, are you? Eni, I was just--
No. I'm not mad.
But I owe you one.
HI-
FIVE!
Hey, Eni! Get back over here! You and your girlfriend can talk about nail polish some other time!
"Nail polish"! Ha ha! Best diss ever!

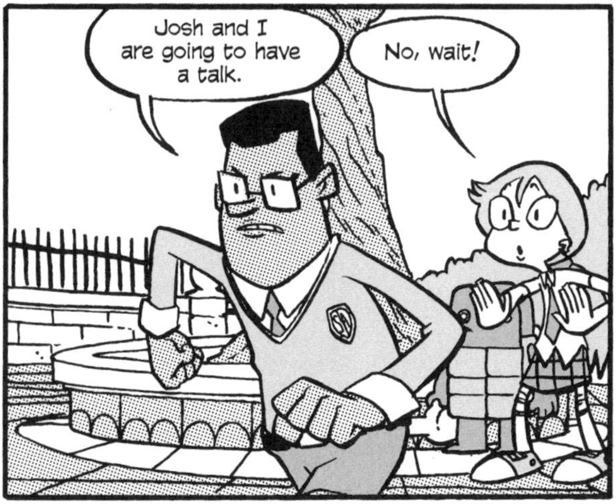
Josh and I
are going to have
a talk.
No, wait!

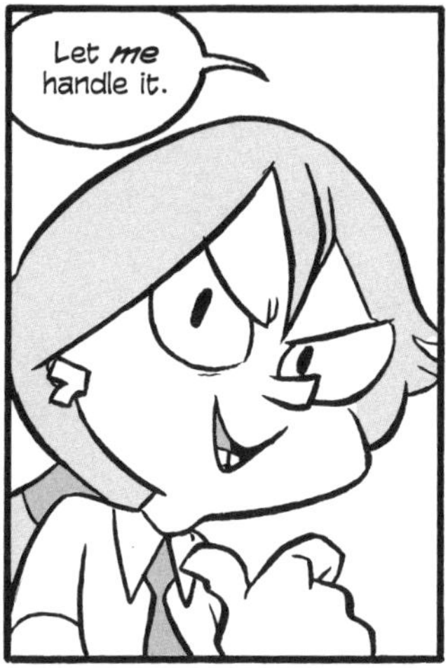
Let *me*
handle it.

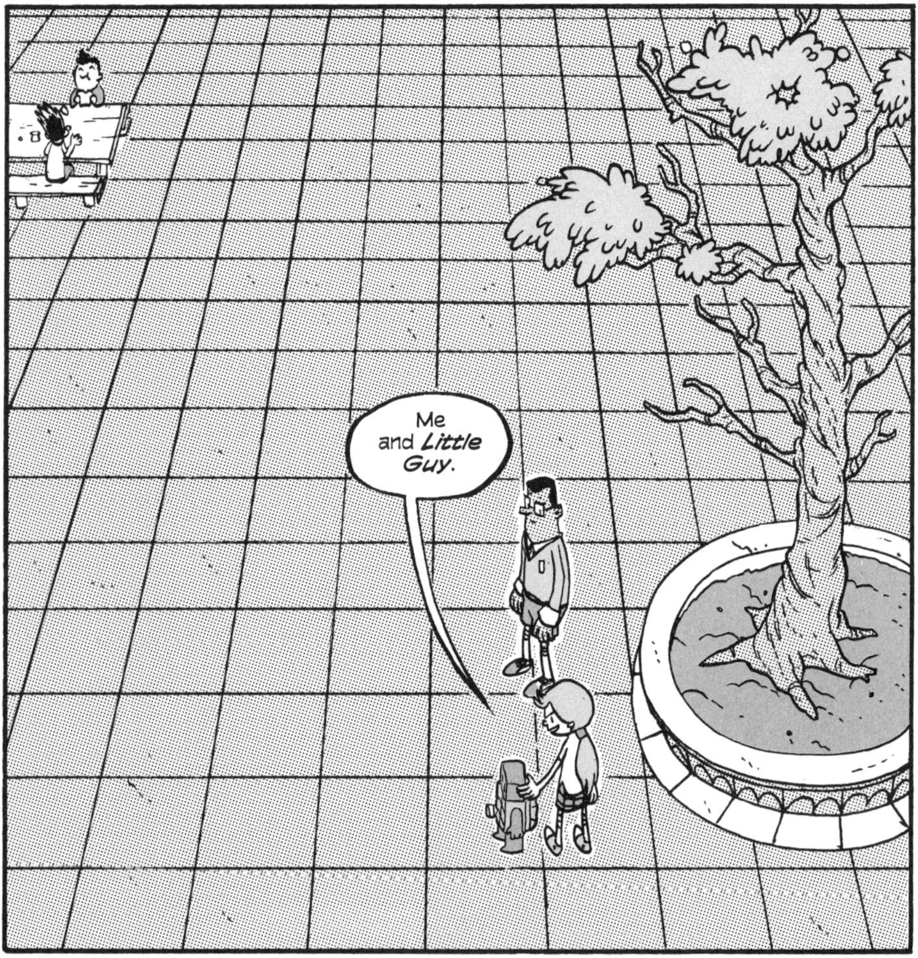
Me
and *Little*
Guy.

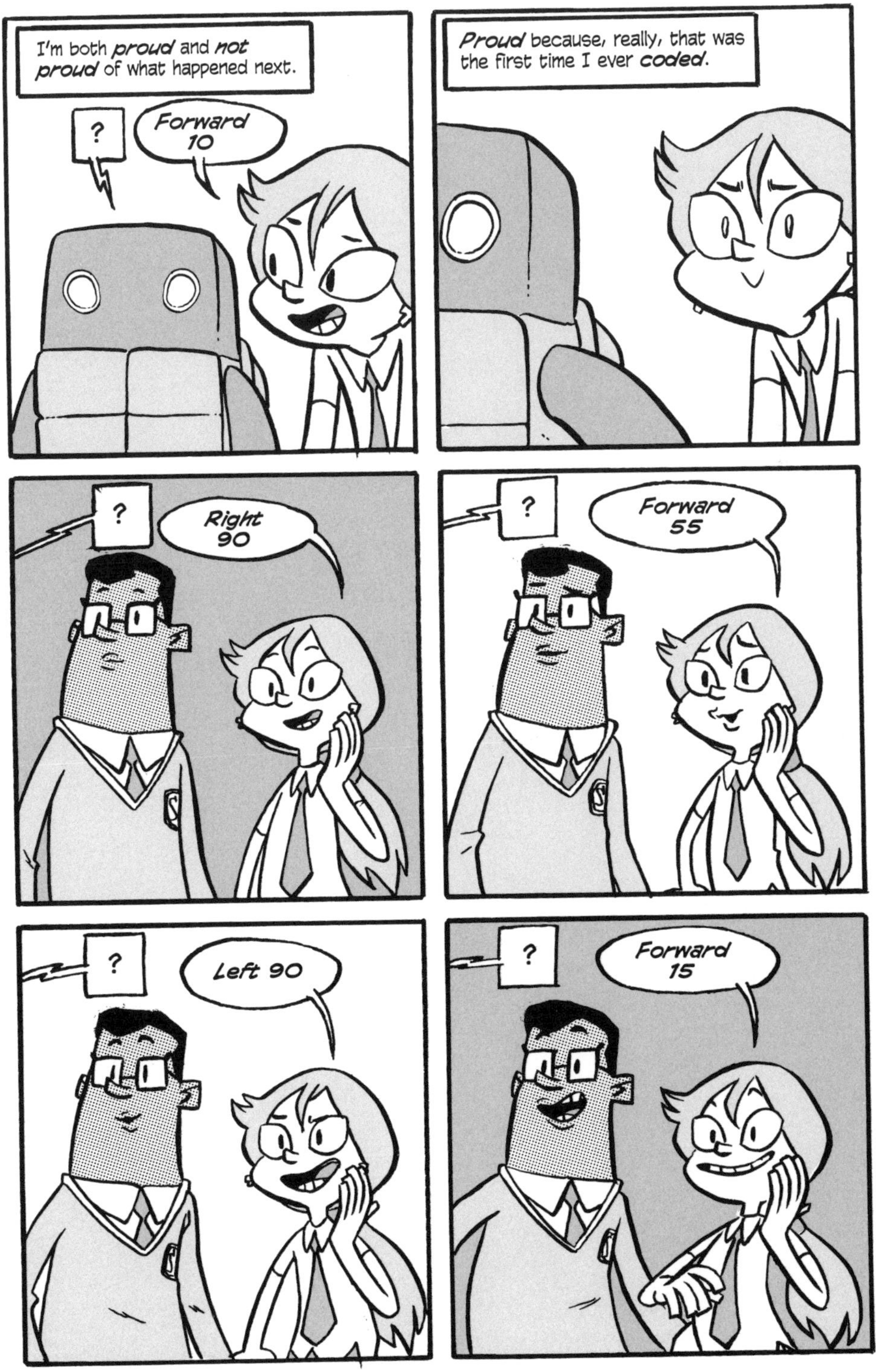
I'm both *proud* and *not proud* of what happened next.
?
Forward 10
Proud because, really, that was the first time I ever *coded*.
?
Right 90
?
Forward 55
?
Left 90
?
Forward 15

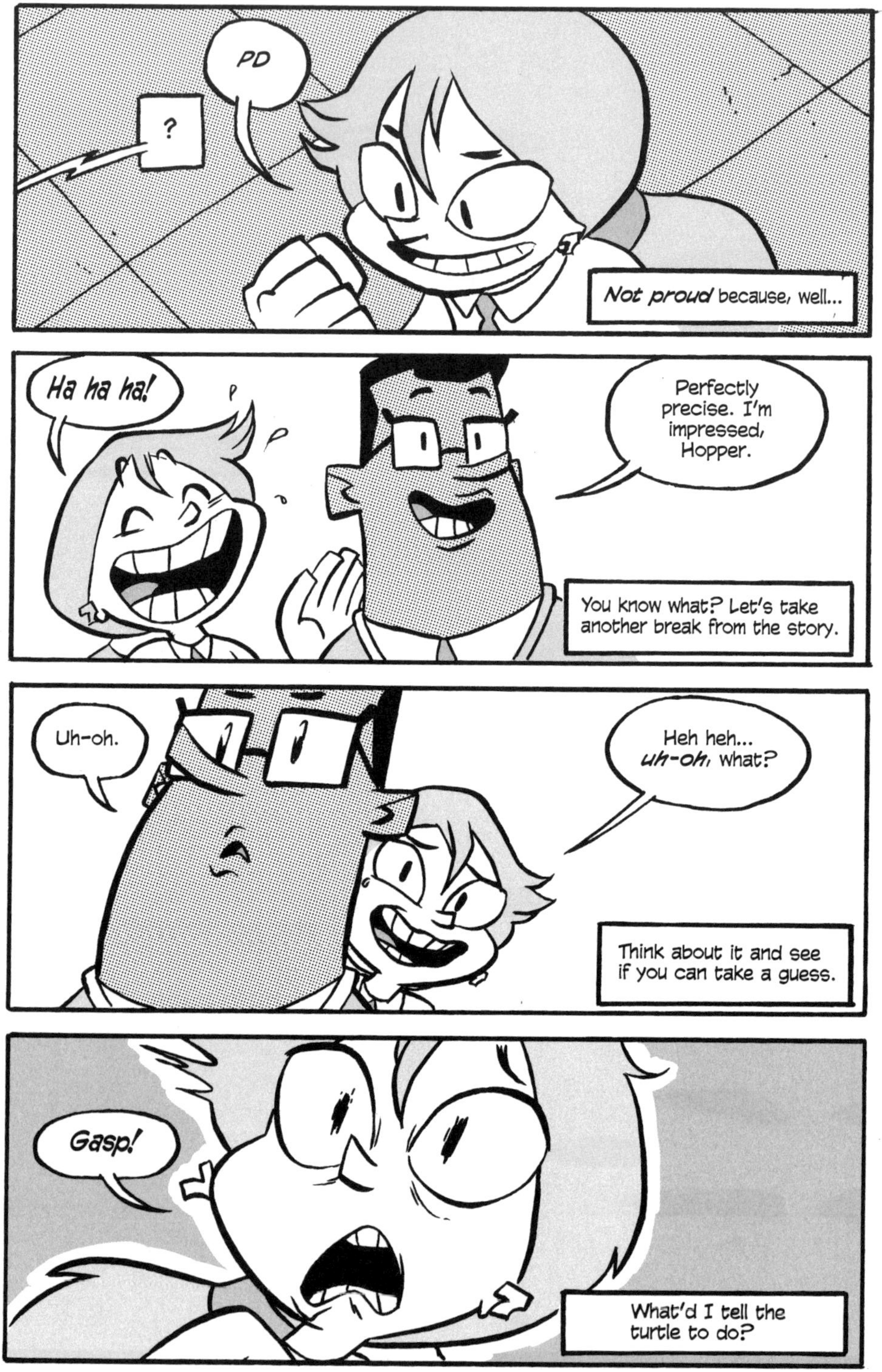
PD
?
Not proud because, well...
Ha ha ha!
Perfectly precise. I'm impressed, Hopper.
You know what? Let's take another break from the story.
Uh-oh.
Heh heh... uh-oh, what?
Think about it and see if you can take a guess.
Gasp!
What'd I tell the turtle to do?

Chapter

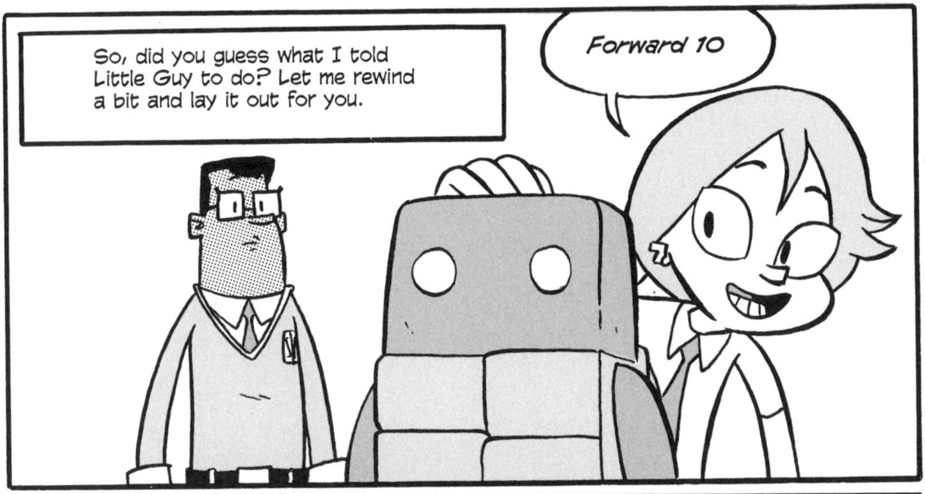
So, did you guess what I told Little Guy to do? Let me rewind a bit and lay it out for you.
Forward 10

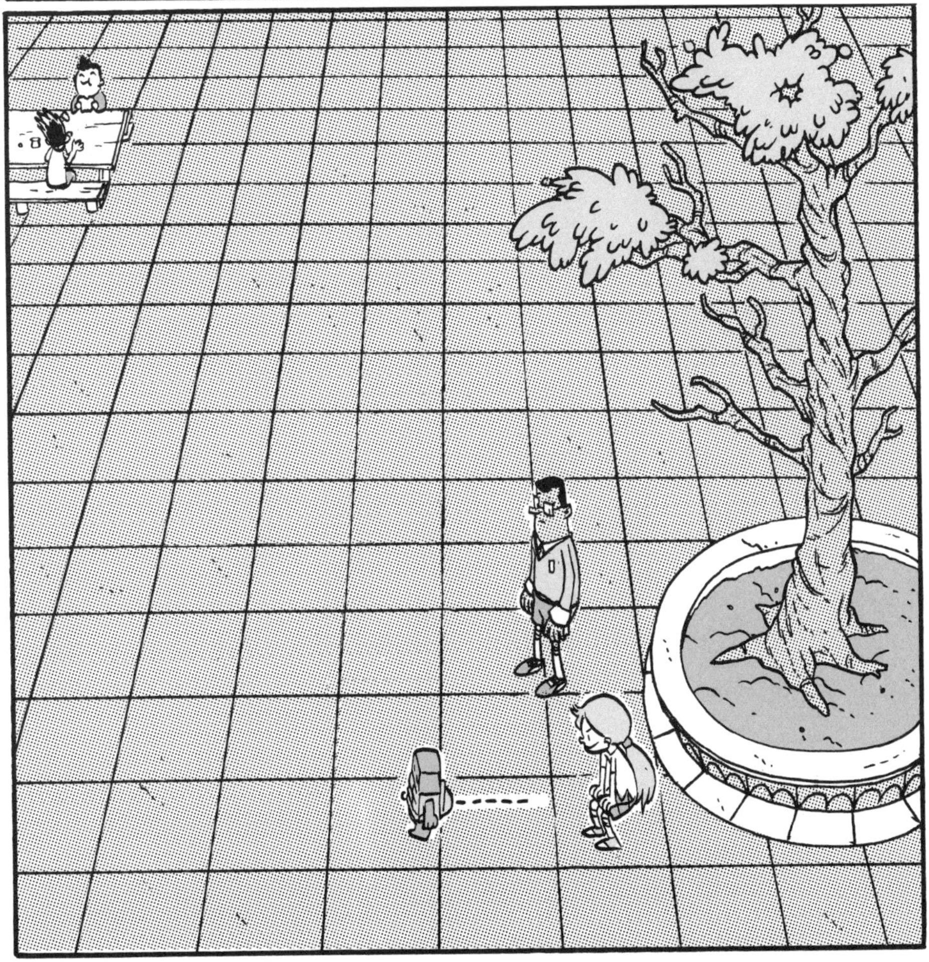

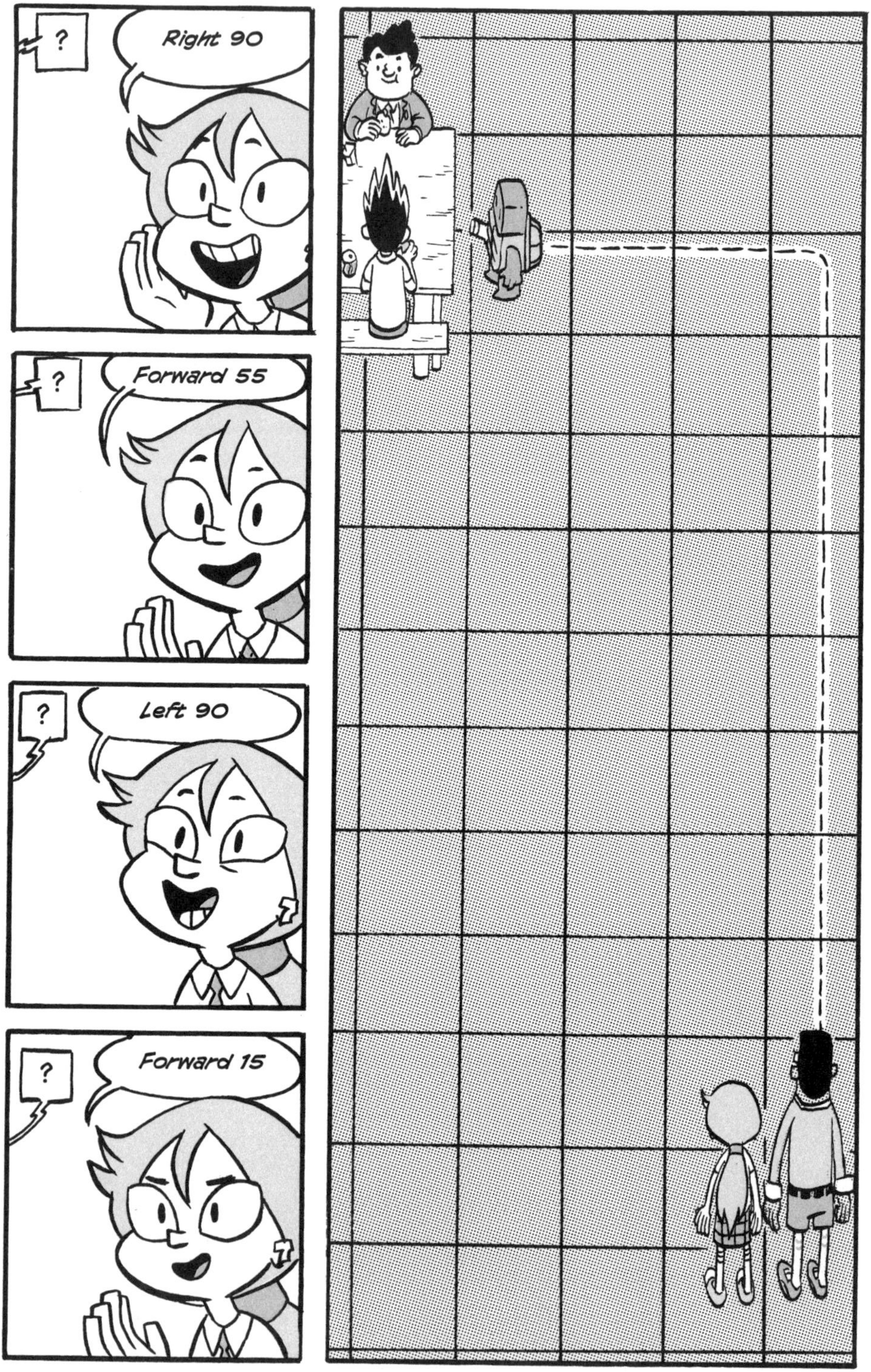
?
Right 90
?
Forward 55
?
Left 90
?
Forward 15

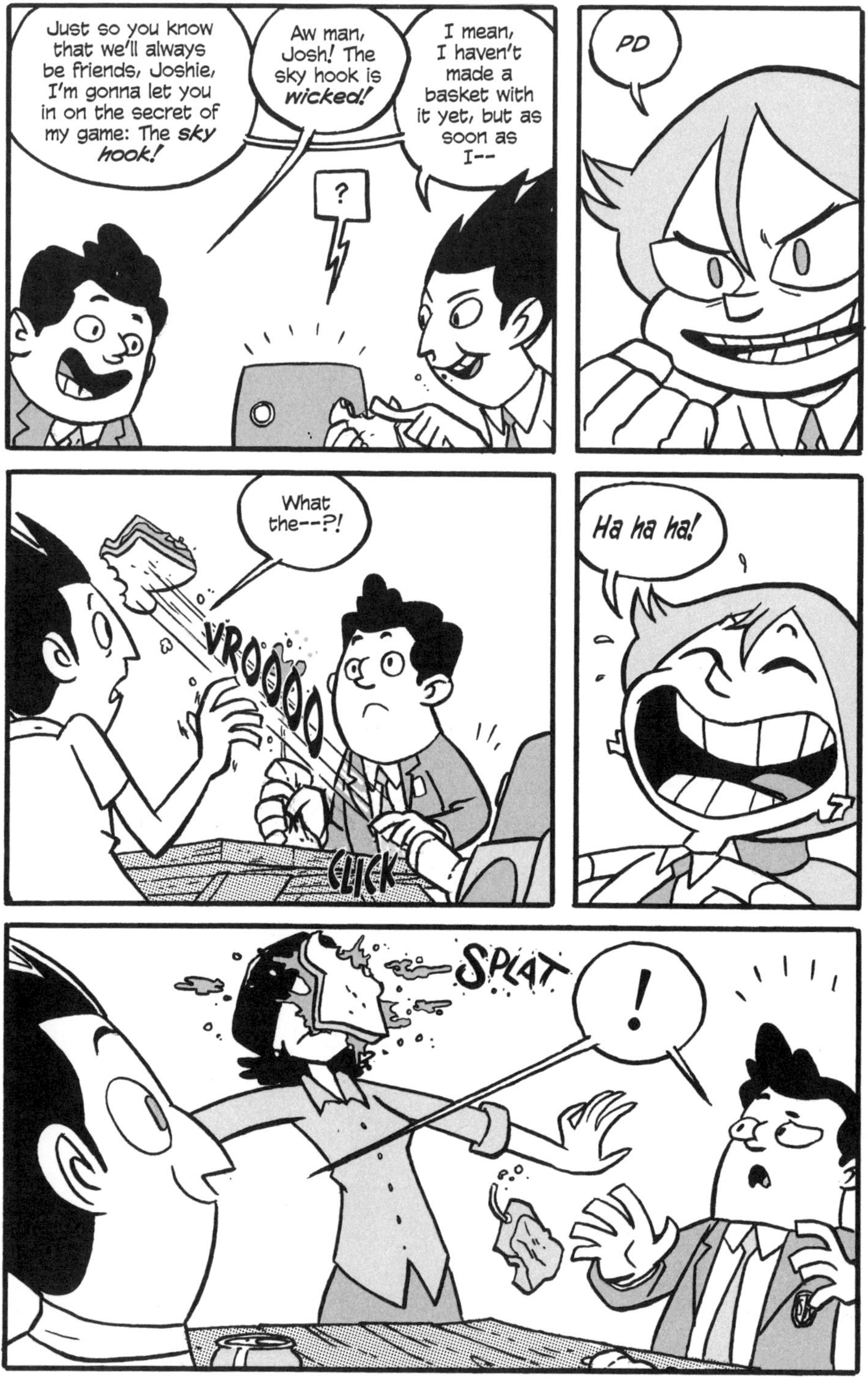
Just so you know that we'll always be friends, Joshie, I'm gonna let you in on the secret of my game: The *sky hook!*
Aw man, Josh! The sky hook is *wicked!*
I mean, I haven't made a basket with it yet, but as soon as I--
?
PD
What the--?!
VROOOOO
CLICK
Ha ha ha!
SPLAT
!

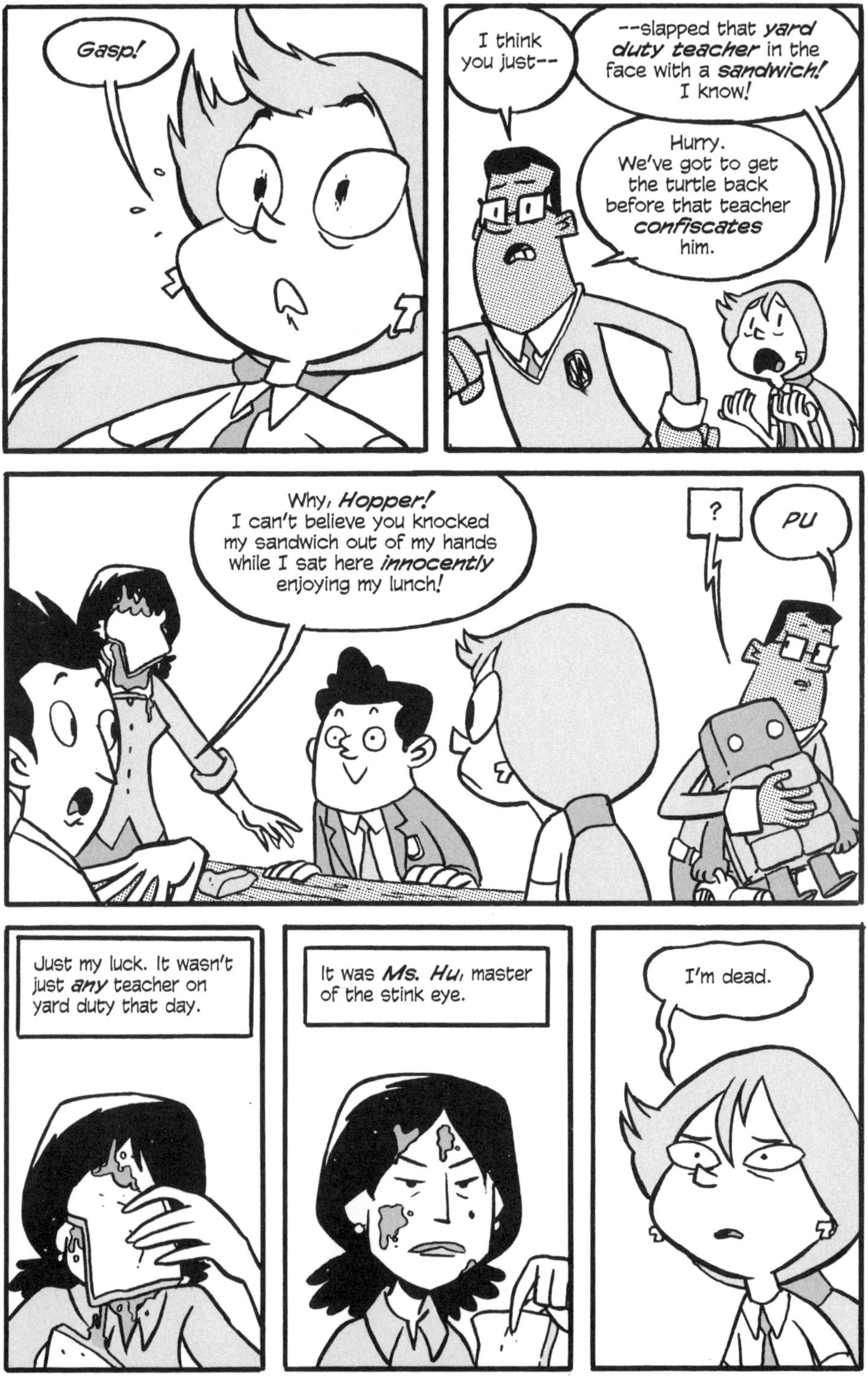

Gasp!
I think you just--
--slapped that *yard duty teacher* in the face with a *sandwich!* I know!
Hurry. We've got to get the turtle back before that teacher *confiscates* him.
Why, *Hopper!* I can't believe you knocked my sandwich out of my hands while I sat here *innocently* enjoying my lunch!
?
PU
Just my luck. It wasn't just *any* teacher on yard duty that day.
It was *Ms. Hu*, master of the stink eye.
I'm dead.

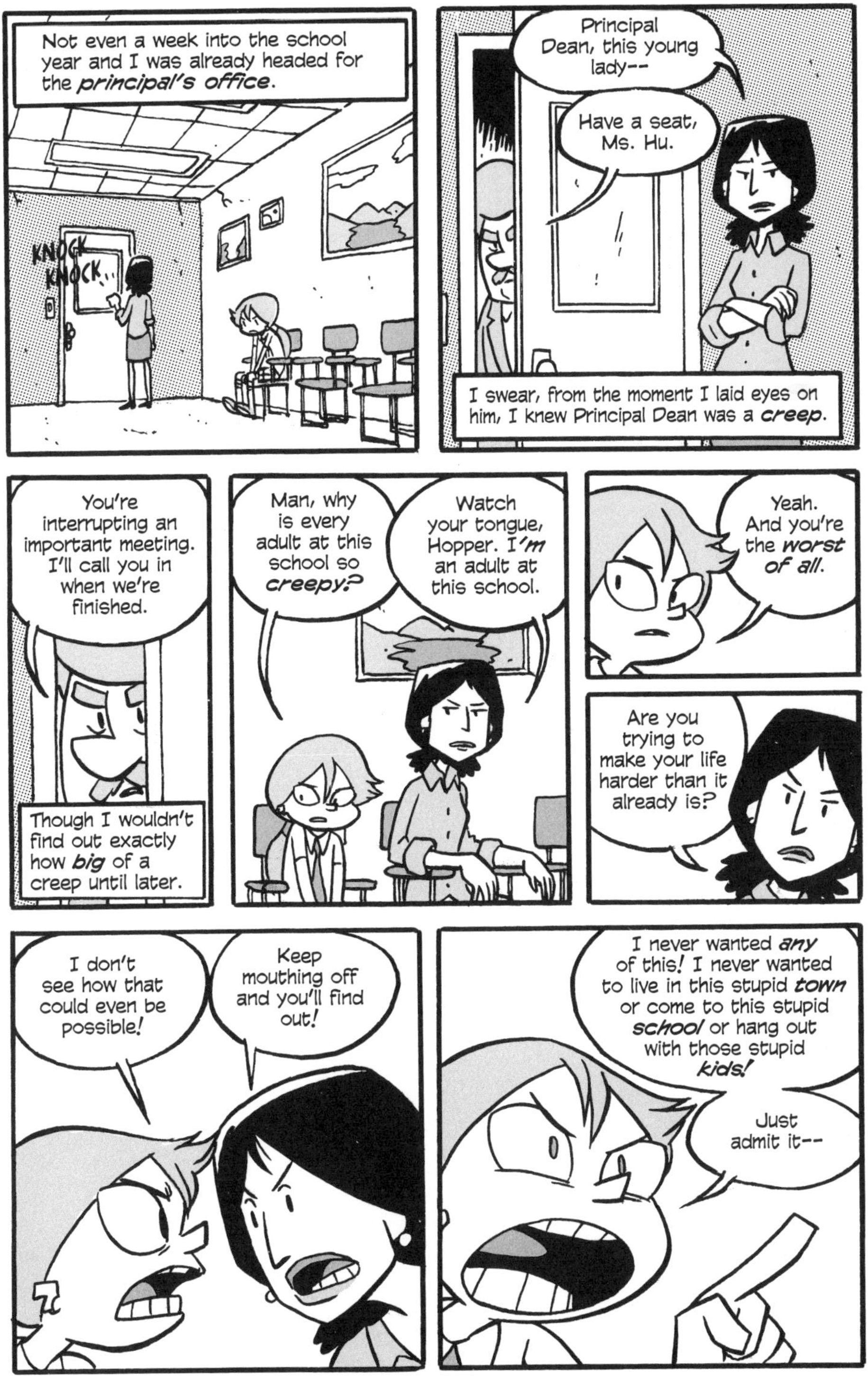

Not even a week into the school year and I was already headed for the *principal's office*.
KNOCK KNOCK
Principal Dean, this young lady--
Have a seat, Ms. Hu.
I swear, from the moment I laid eyes on him, I knew Principal Dean was a *creep*.
You're interrupting an important meeting. I'll call you in when we're finished.
Though I wouldn't find out exactly how *big* of a creep until later.
Man, why is every adult at this school so *creepy?*
Watch your tongue, Hopper. *I'm* an adult at this school.
Yeah. And you're the *worst of all*.
Are you trying to make your life harder than it already is?
I don't see how that could even be possible!
Keep mouthing off and you'll find out!
I never wanted *any* of this! I never wanted to live in this stupid *town* or come to this stupid *school* or hang out with those stupid *kids!*
Just admit it--

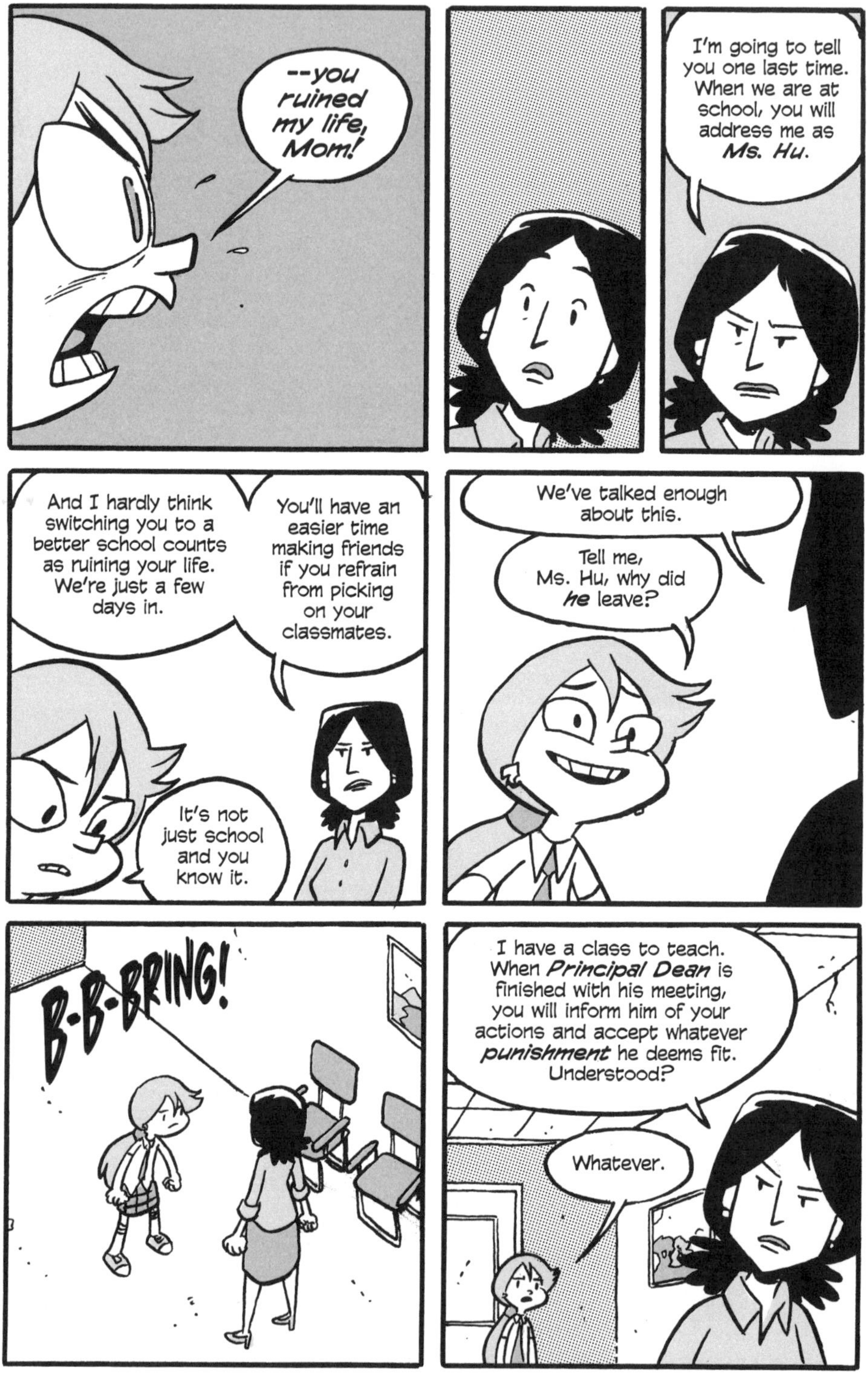
--you ruined my life, Mom!
I'm going to tell you one last time. When we are at school, you will address me as *Ms. Hu*.
And I hardly think switching you to a better school counts as ruining your life. We're just a few days in.
You'll have an easier time making friends if you refrain from picking on your classmates.
It's not just school and you know it.
We've talked enough about this.
Tell me, Ms. Hu, why did *he* leave?
B-B-BRING!
I have a class to teach. When *Principal Dean* is finished with his meeting, you will inform him of your actions and accept whatever *punishment* he deems fit. Understood?
Whatever.

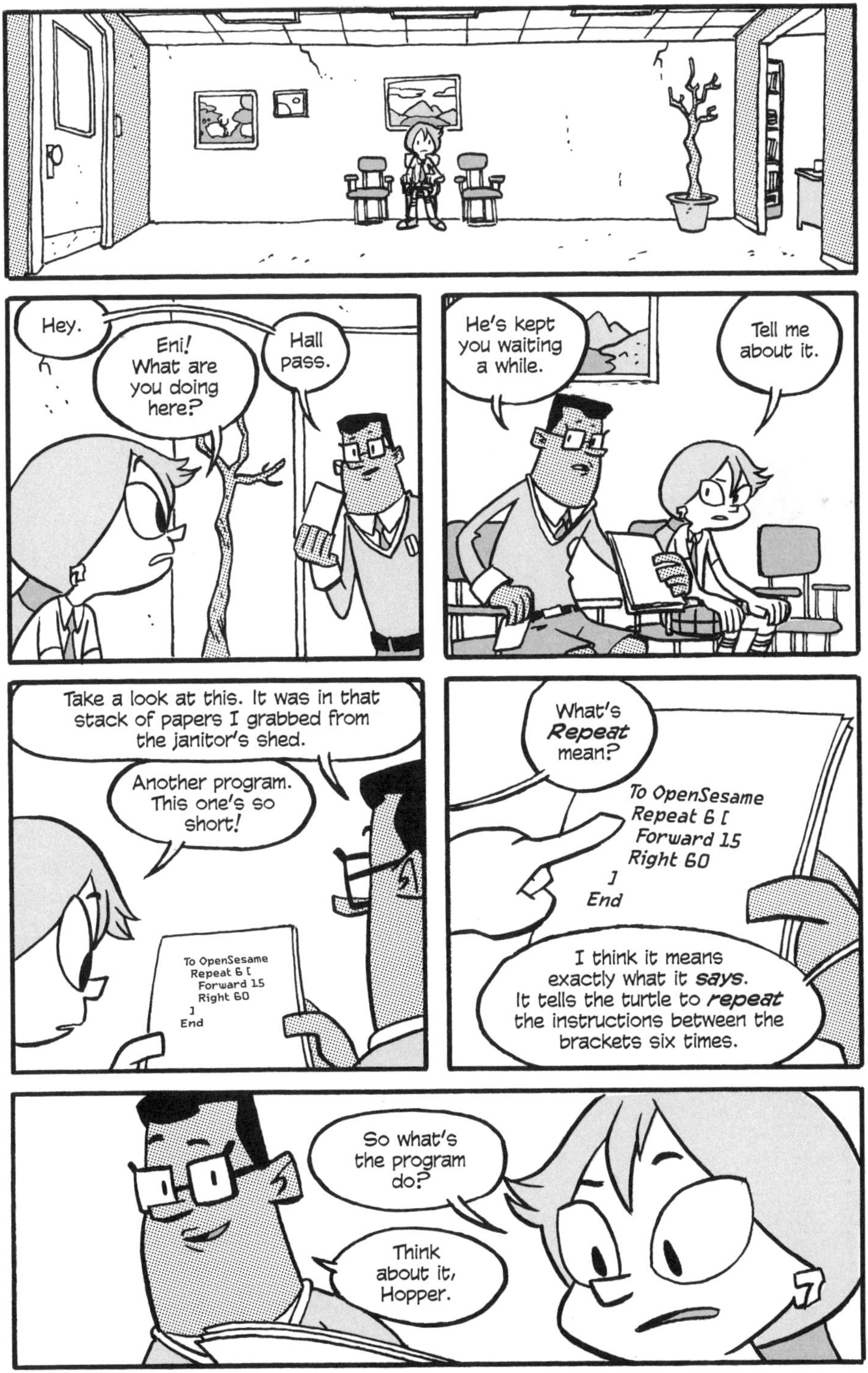
Hey.
Eni! What are you doing here?
Hall pass.
He's kept you waiting a while.
Tell me about it.
Take a look at this. It was in that stack of papers I grabbed from the janitor's shed.
Another program. This one's so short!
To OpenSesame
Repeat 6 [
Forward 15
Right 60
]
End
What's *Repeat* mean?
To OpenSesame
Repeat 6 [
Forward 15
Right 60
]
End
I think it means exactly what it *says*. It tells the turtle to *repeat* the instructions between the brackets six times.
So what's the program do?
Think about it, Hopper.

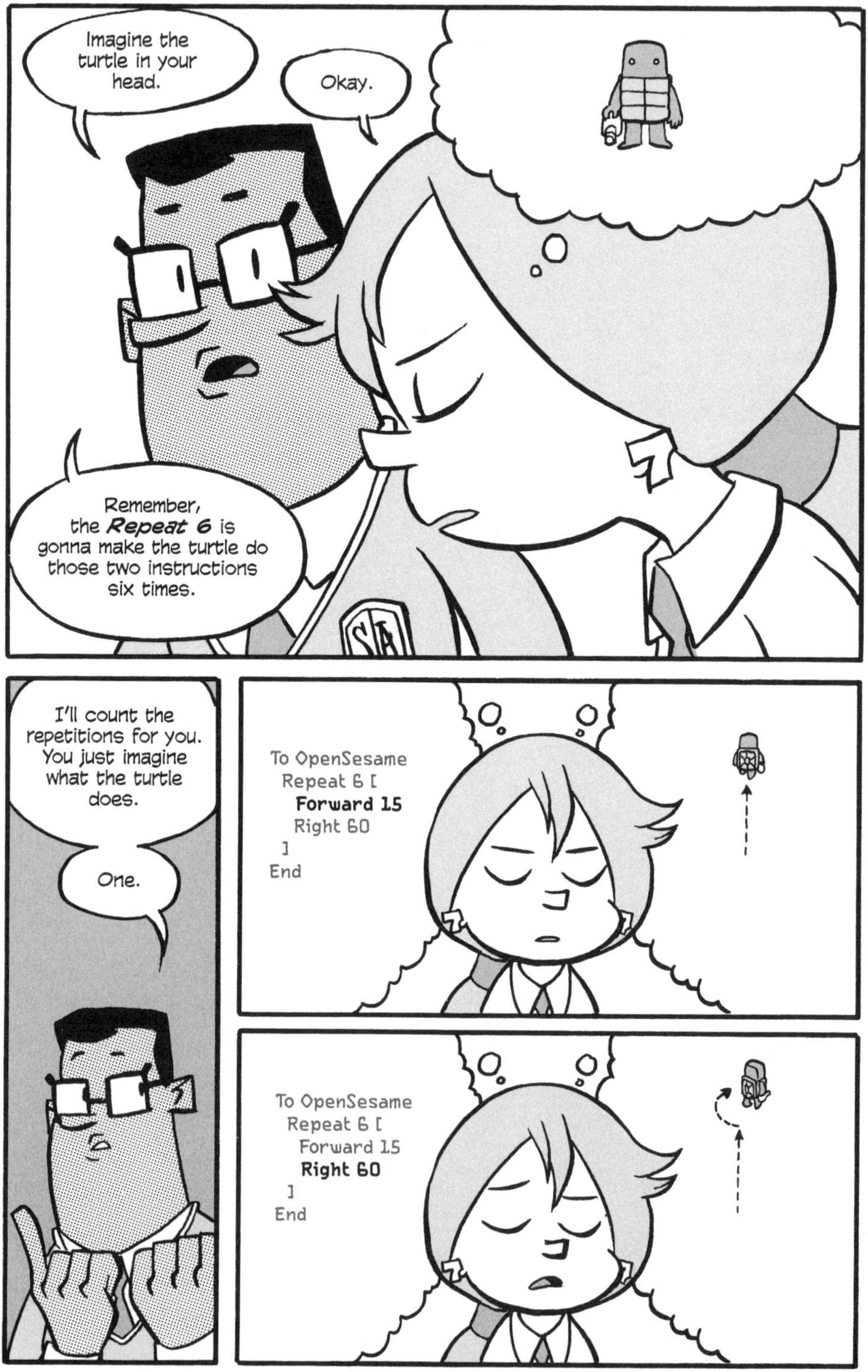

Imagine the turtle in your head.
Okay.
Remember, the *Repeat 6* is gonna make the turtle do those two instructions six times.
I'll count the repetitions for you. You just imagine what the turtle does.
One.
To OpenSesame
Repeat 6 [
Forward 15
Right 60
]
End
To OpenSesame
Repeat 6 [
Forward 15
Right 60
]
End

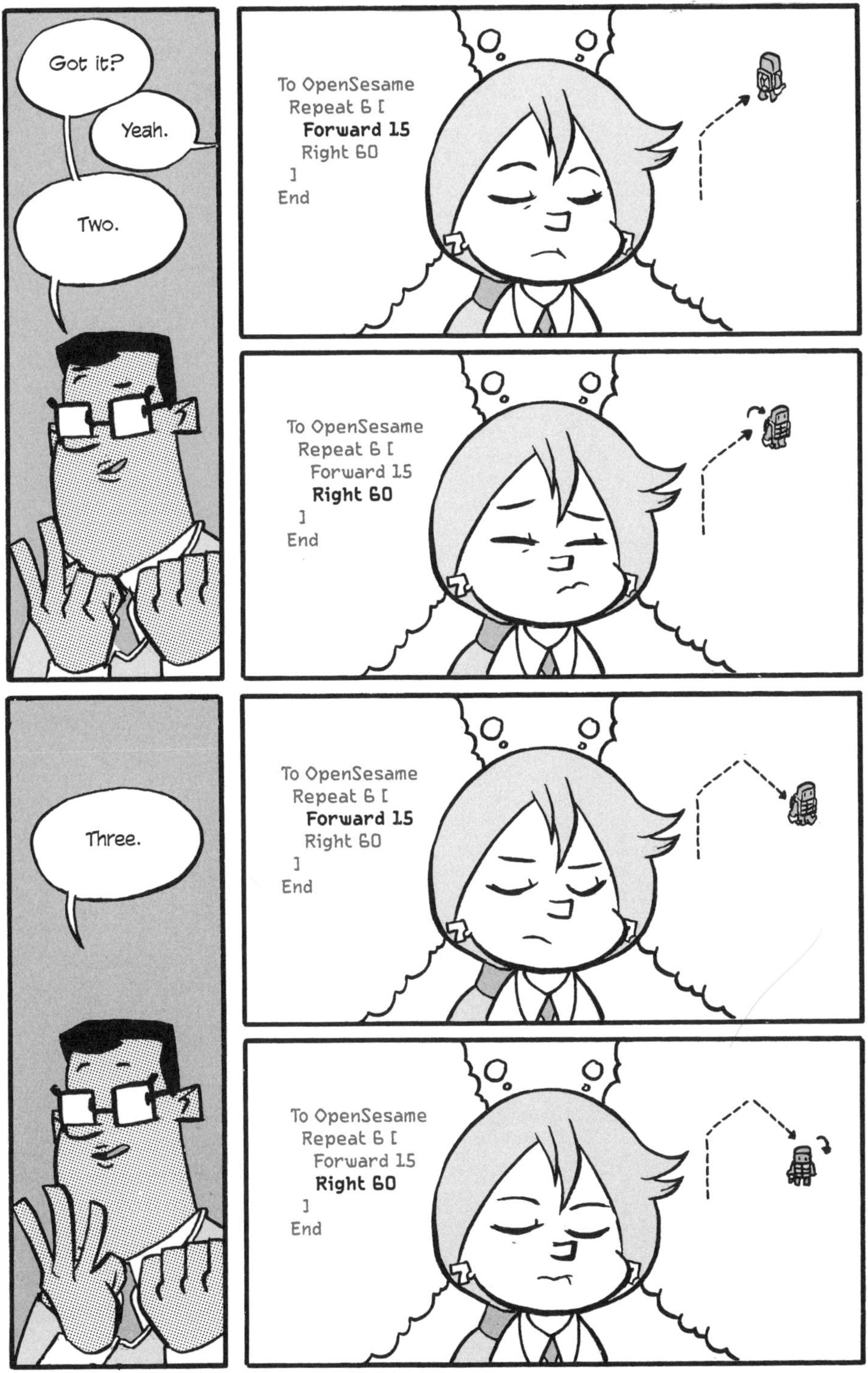
Got it?
Yeah.
Two.
To OpenSesame
Repeat 6 [
Forward 15
Right 60
]
End
To OpenSesame
Repeat 6 [
Forward 15
Right 60
]
End
Three.
To OpenSesame
Repeat 6 [
Forward 15
Right 60
]
End
To OpenSesame
Repeat 6 [
Forward 15
Right 60
]
End

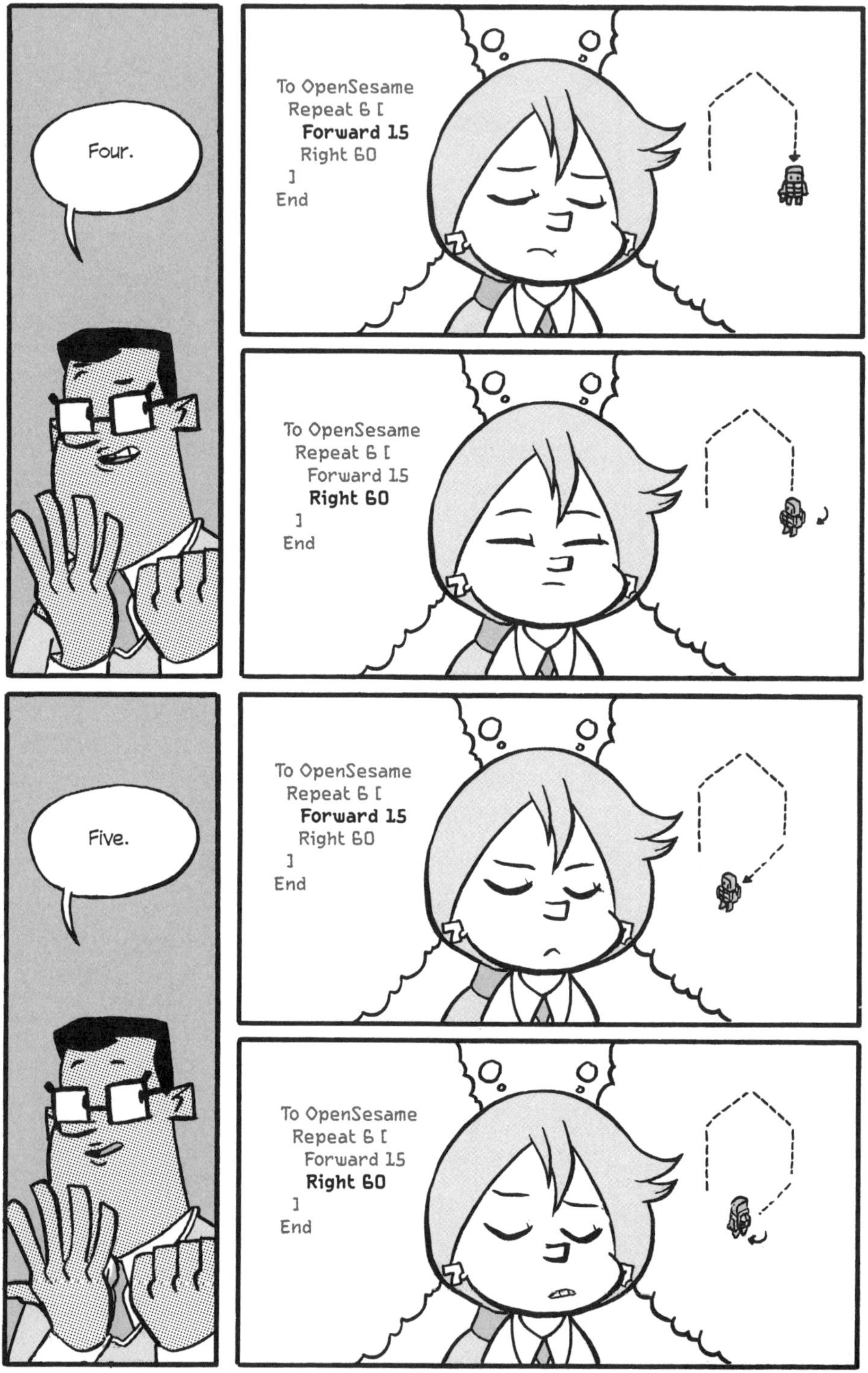
Four.
To OpenSesame
Repeat 6 [
Forward 15
Right 60
]
End
To OpenSesame
Repeat 6 [
Forward 15
Right 60
]
End
Five.
To OpenSesame
Repeat 6 [
Forward 15
Right 60
]
End
To OpenSesame
Repeat 6 [
Forward 15
Right 60
]
End

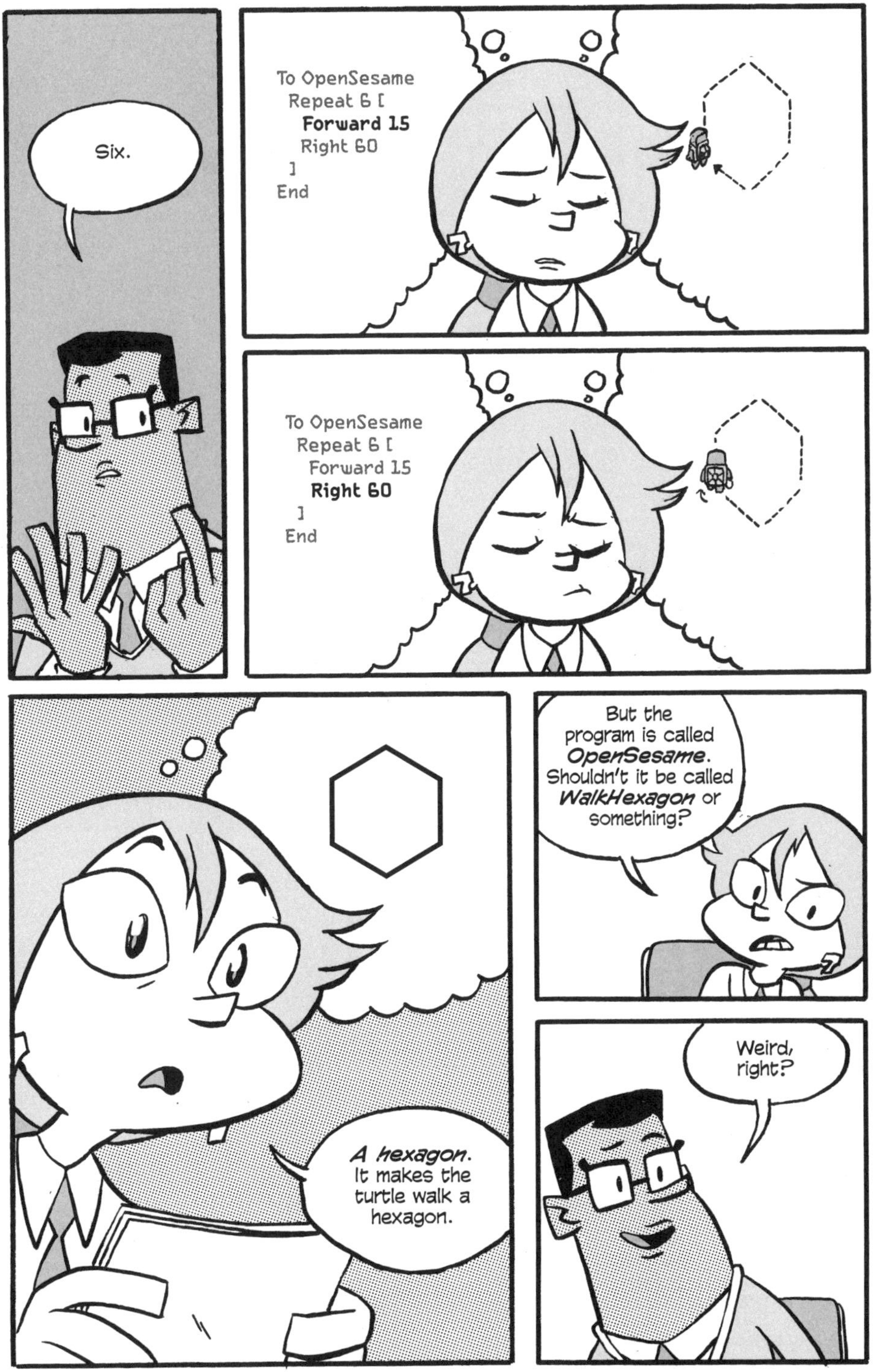

Six.
To OpenSesame
Repeat 6 [
Forward 15
Right 60
]
End
To OpenSesame
Repeat 6 [
Forward 15
Right 60
]
End
A hexagon. It makes the turtle walk a hexagon.
But the program is called *OpenSesame*. Shouldn't it be called *WalkHexagon* or something?
Weird, right?

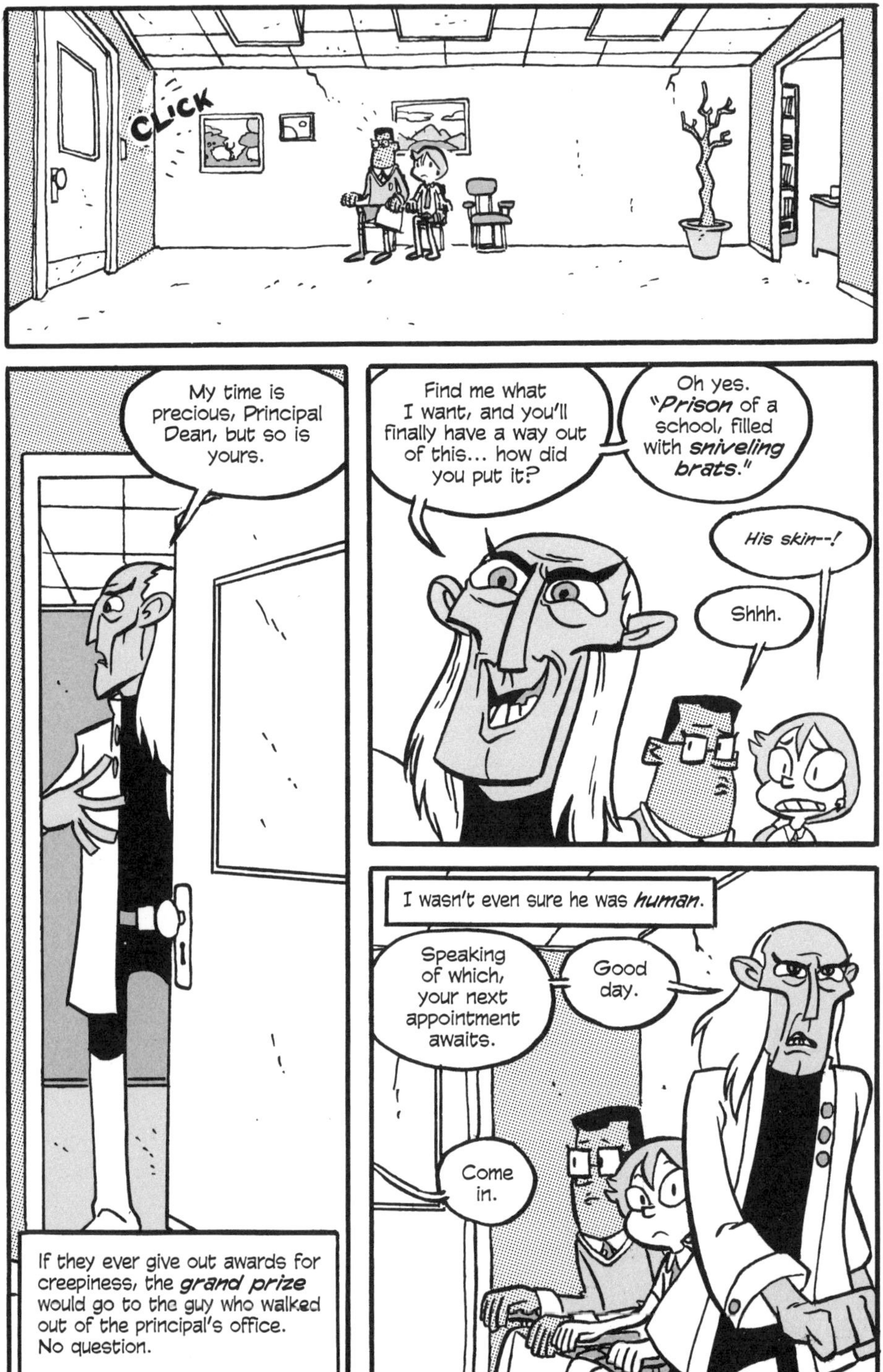

CLICK
My time is precious, Principal Dean, but so is yours.
If they ever give out awards for creepiness, the *grand prize* would go to the guy who walked out of the principal's office. No question.
Find me what I want, and you'll finally have a way out of this... how did you put it?
Oh yes. "*Prison* of a school, filled with *sniveling brats*."
His skin--!
Shhh.
I wasn't even sure he was *human*.
Speaking of which, your next appointment awaits.
Good day.
Come in.

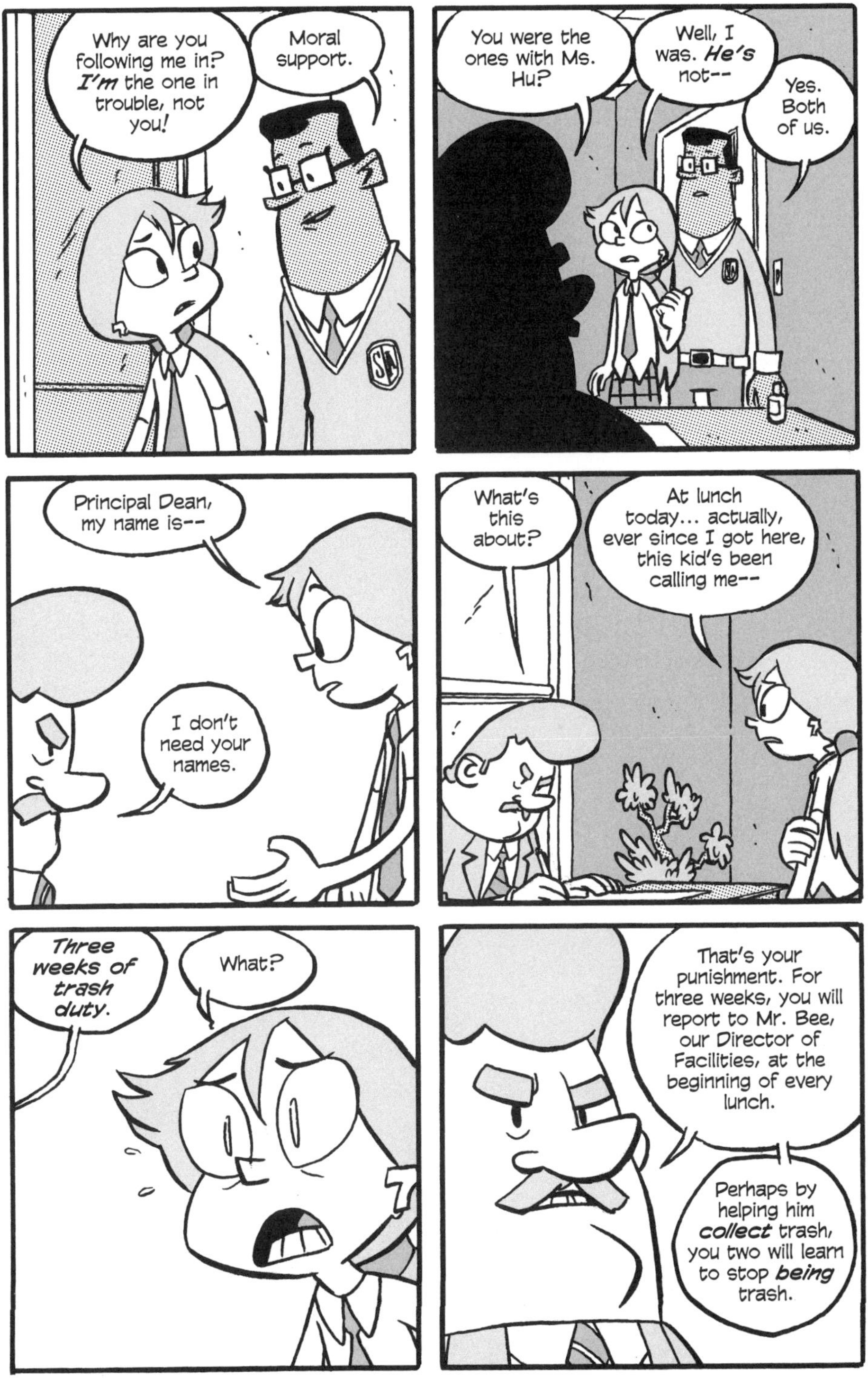
Why are you following me in? *I'm* the one in trouble, not you!
Moral support.
You were the ones with Ms. Hu?
Well, I was. *He's* not--
Yes. Both of us.
Principal Dean, my name is--
I don't need your names.
What's this about?
At lunch today... actually, ever since I got here, this kid's been calling me--
Three weeks of trash duty.
What?
That's your punishment. For three weeks, you will report to Mr. Bee, our Director of Facilities, at the beginning of every lunch.
Perhaps by helping him *collect* trash, you two will learn to stop *being* trash.

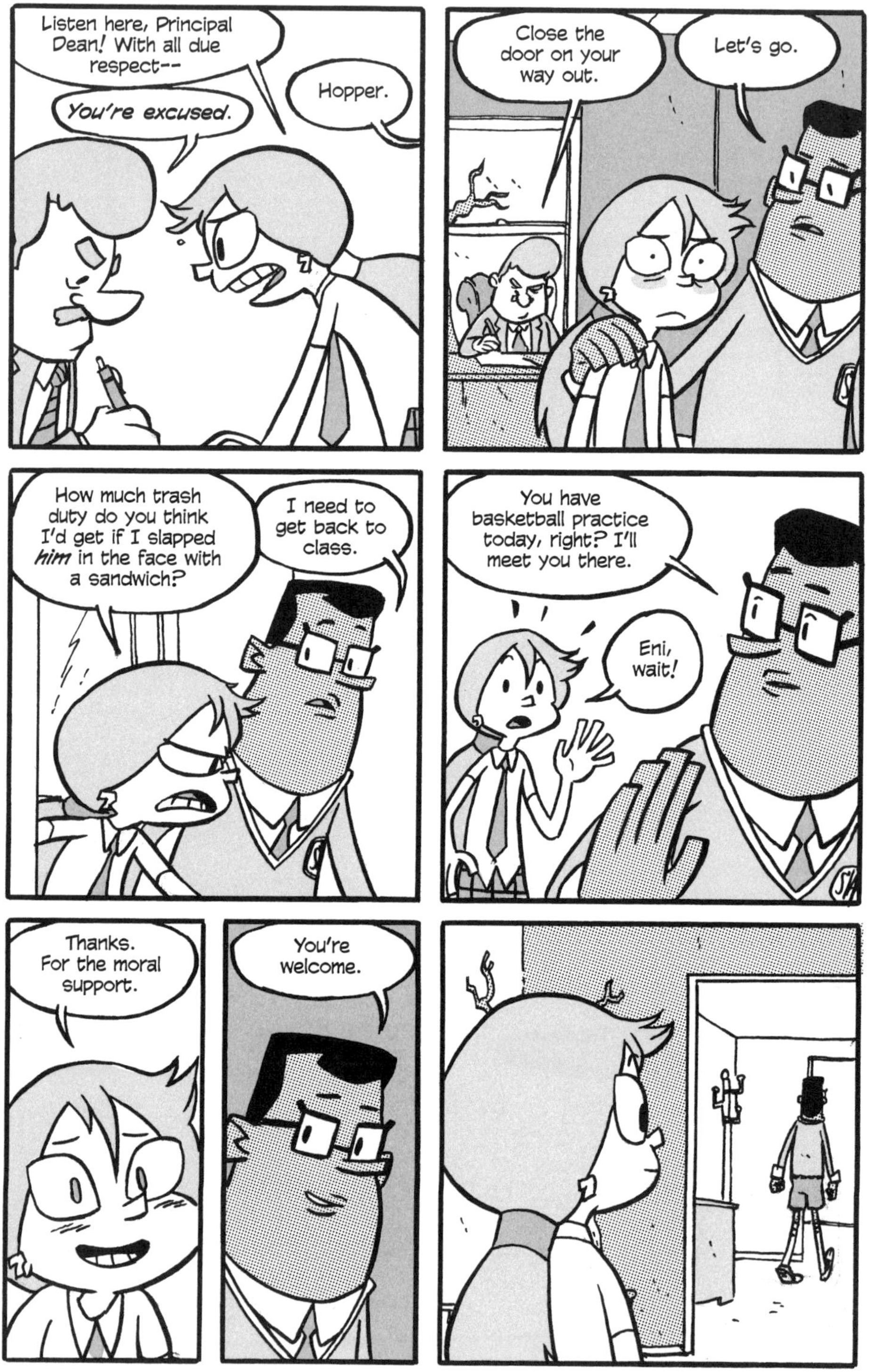

Listen here, Principal Dean! With all due respect--
You're excused.
Hopper.
Close the door on your way out.
Let's go.
How much trash duty do you think I'd get if I slapped *him* in the face with a sandwich?
I need to get back to class.
You have basketball practice today, right? I'll meet you there.
Eni, wait!
Thanks. For the moral support.
You're welcome.

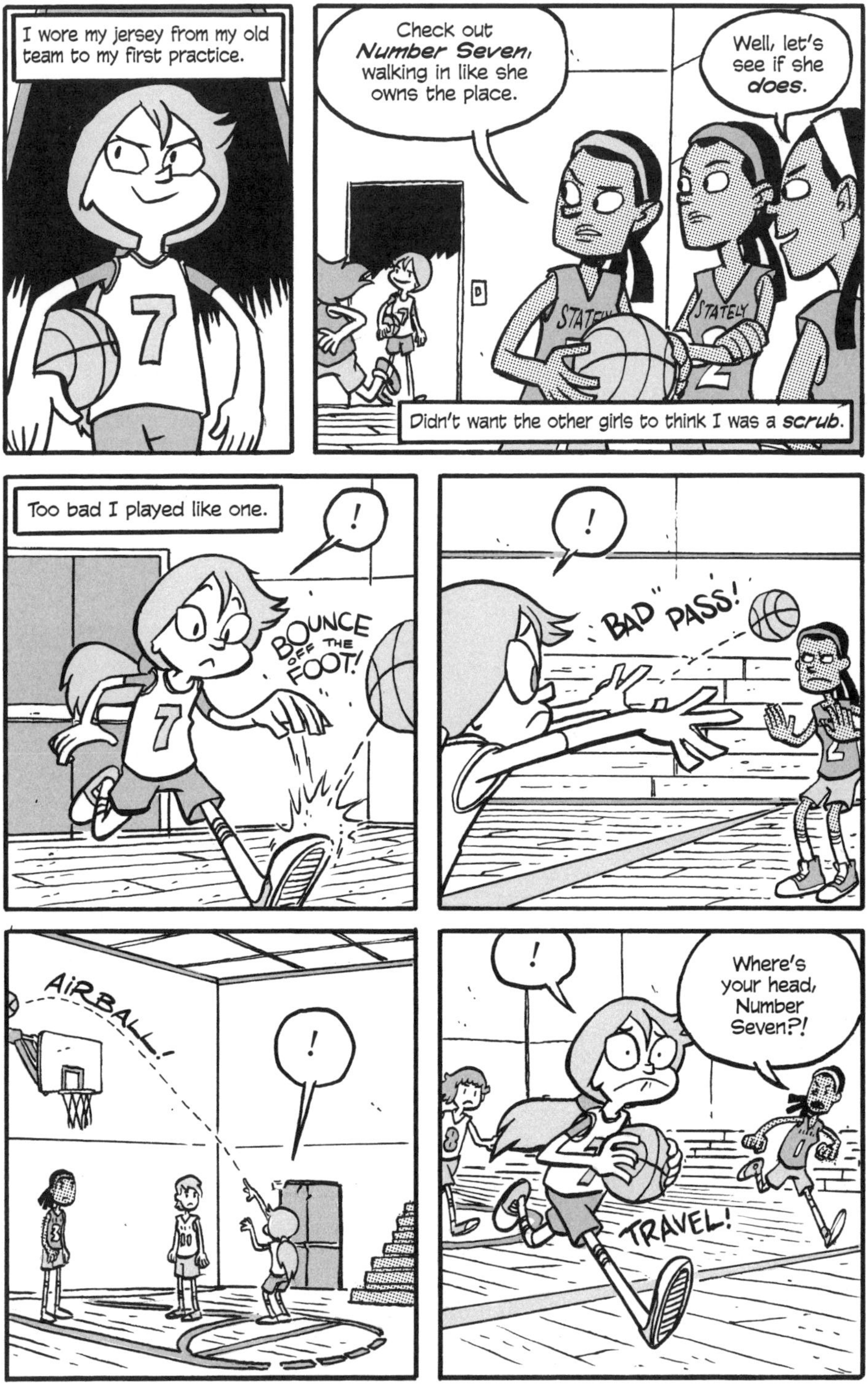

I wore my jersey from my old team to my first practice.
Check out Number Seven, walking in like she owns the place.
Well, let's see if she does.
STATELY
STATELY
Didn't want the other girls to think I was a scrub.
Too bad I played like one.
!
BOUNCE OFF THE FOOT!
!
BAD PASS!
AIRBALL!
!
!
Where's your head, Number Seven?!
TRAVEL!

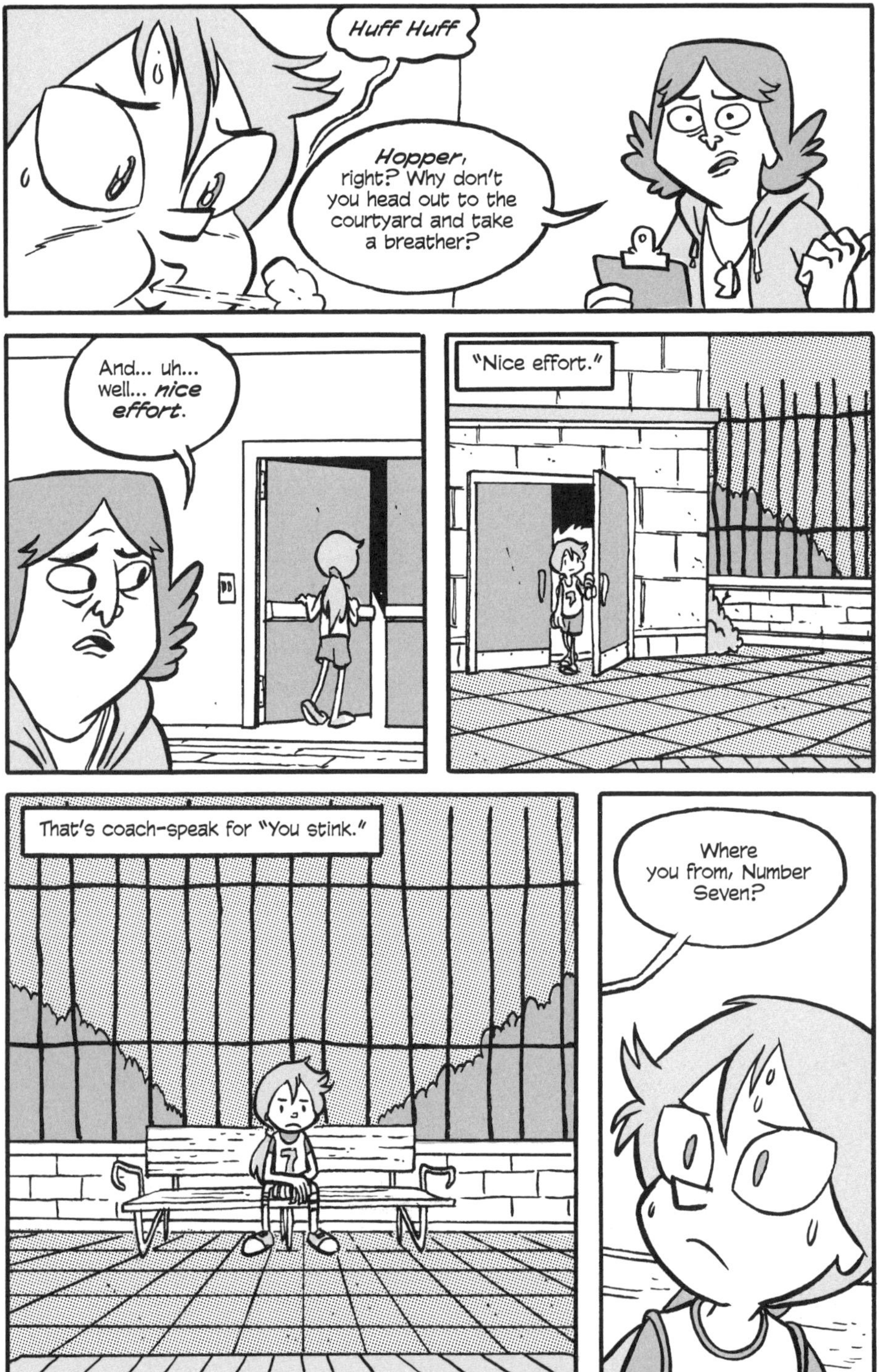
Huff Huff
Hopper, right? Why don't you head out to the courtyard and take a breather?
And... uh... well... nice effort.
"Nice effort."
That's coach-speak for "You stink."
Where you from, Number Seven?

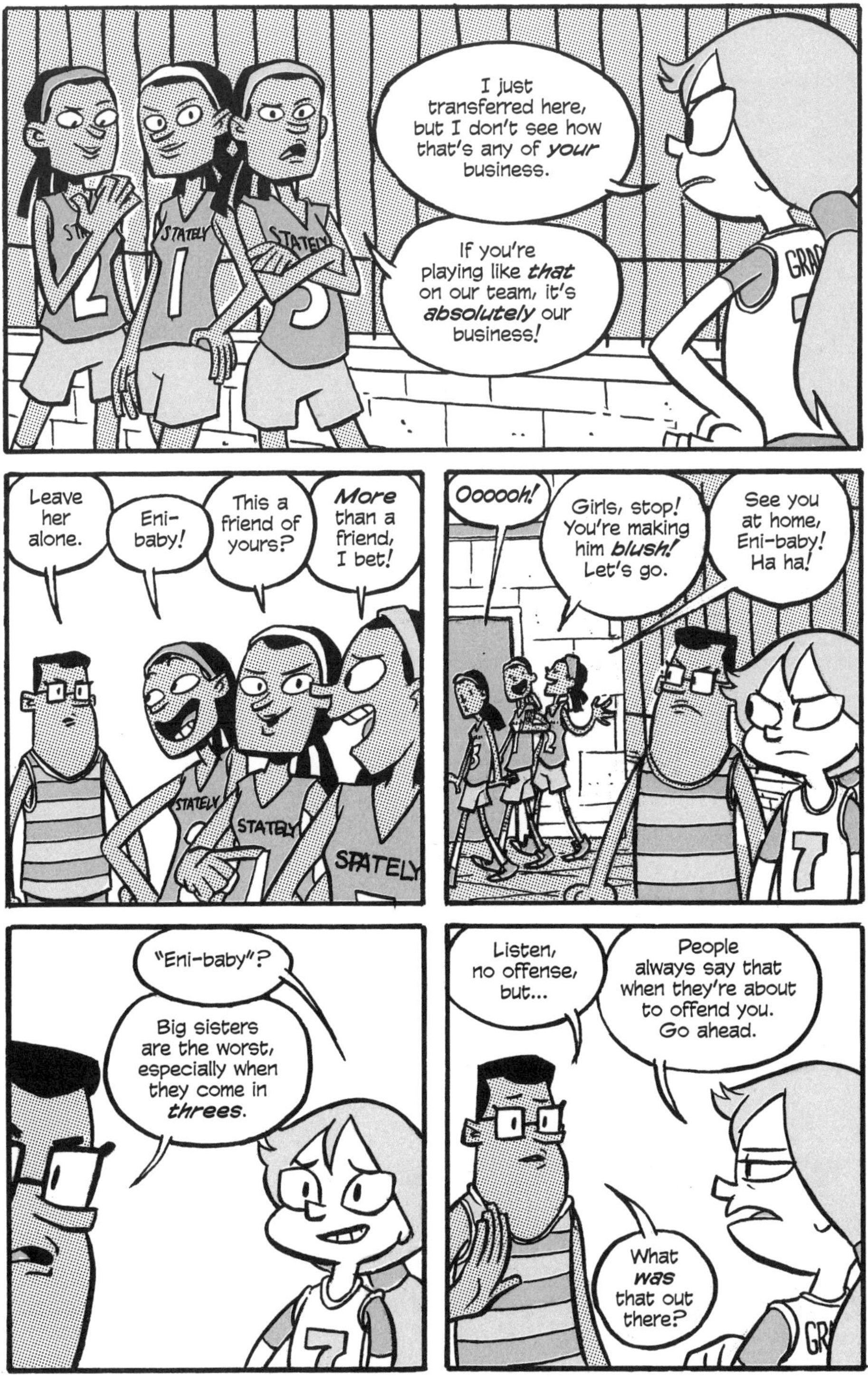

I just transferred here, but I don't see how that's any of *your* business.
If you're playing like *that* on our team, it's *absolutely* our business!
Leave her alone.
Eni-baby!
This a friend of yours?
More than a friend, I bet!
Oooooh!
Girls, stop! You're making him *blush!* Let's go.
See you at home, Eni-baby! Ha ha!
"Eni-baby"?
Big sisters are the worst, especially when they come in *threes*.
Listen, no offense, but...
People always say that when they're about to offend you. Go ahead.
What *was* that out there?

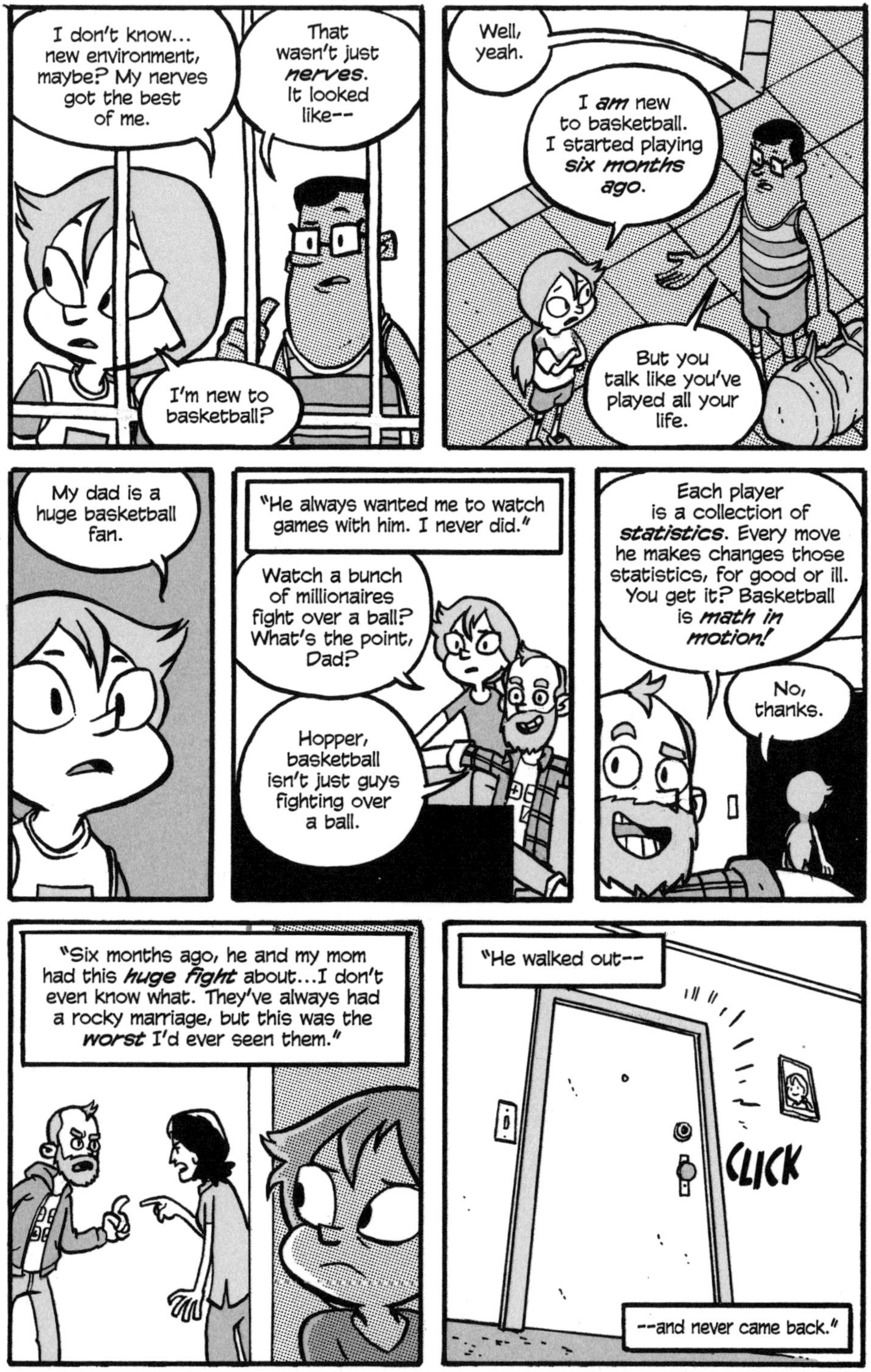

I don't know... new environment, maybe? My nerves got the best of me.
That wasn't just *nerves*. It looked like--
I'm new to basketball?
Well, yeah.
I *am* new to basketball. I started playing *six months ago*.
But you talk like you've played all your life.
My dad is a huge basketball fan.
"He always wanted me to watch games with him. I never did."
Watch a bunch of millionaires fight over a ball? What's the point, Dad?
Hopper, basketball isn't just guys fighting over a ball.
Each player is a collection of *statistics*. Every move he makes changes those statistics, for good or ill. You get it? Basketball is *math in motion!*
No, thanks.
"Six months ago, he and my mom had this *huge fight* about...I don't even know what. They've always had a rocky marriage, but this was the *worst* I'd ever seen them."
"He walked out--
CLICK
--and never came back."

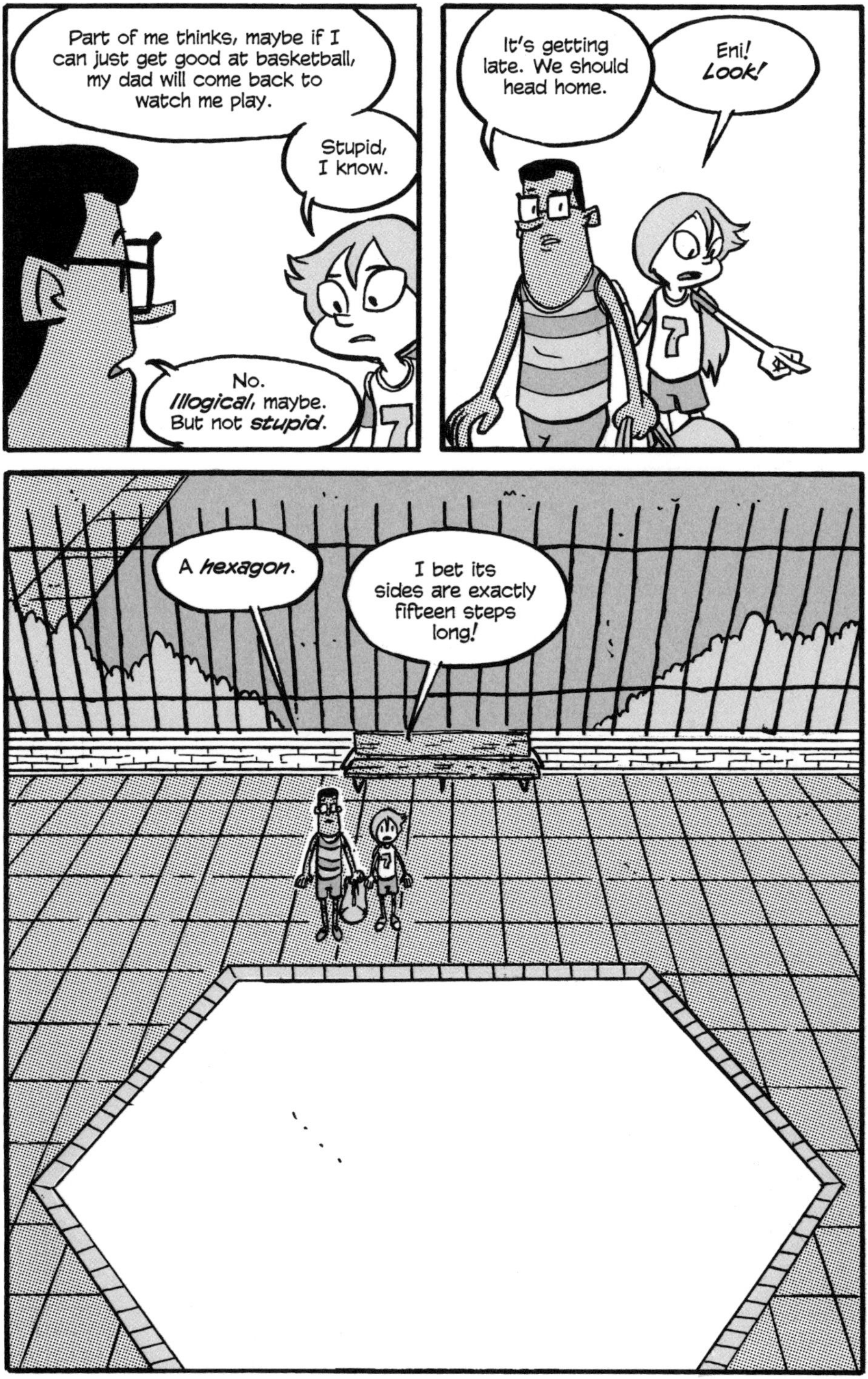
Part of me thinks, maybe if I can just get good at basketball, my dad will come back to watch me play.
Stupid, I know.
No. *Illogical*, maybe. But not *stupid*.
It's getting late. We should head home.
Eni! *Look!*
A *hexagon*.
I bet its sides are exactly fifteen steps long!

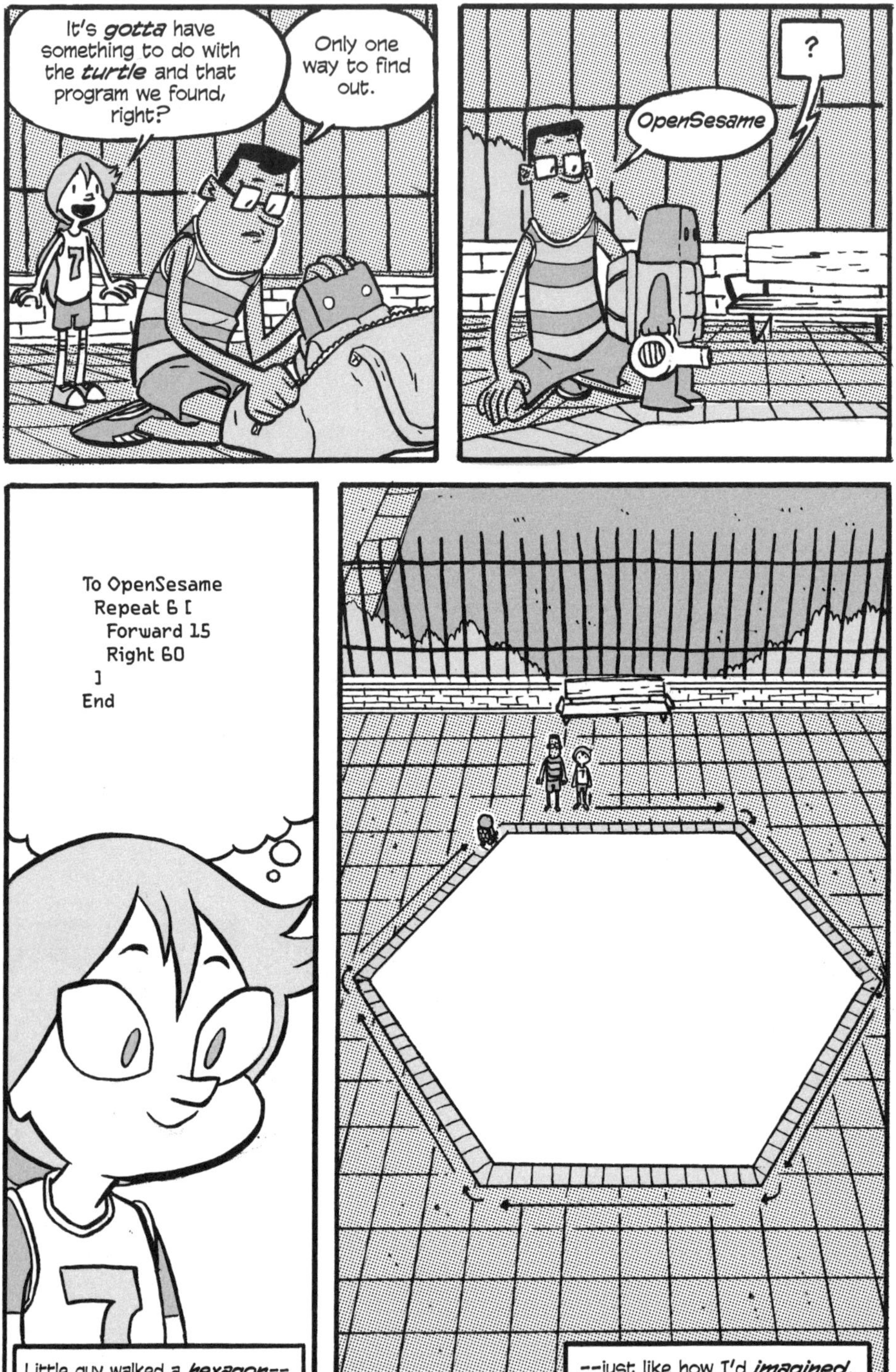
It's *gotta* have something to do with the *turtle* and that program we found, right?
Only one way to find out.
OpenSesame
?
To OpenSesame
Repeat 6 [
Forward 15
Right 60
]
End
Little guy walked a *hexagon*--
--just like how I'd *imagined*.

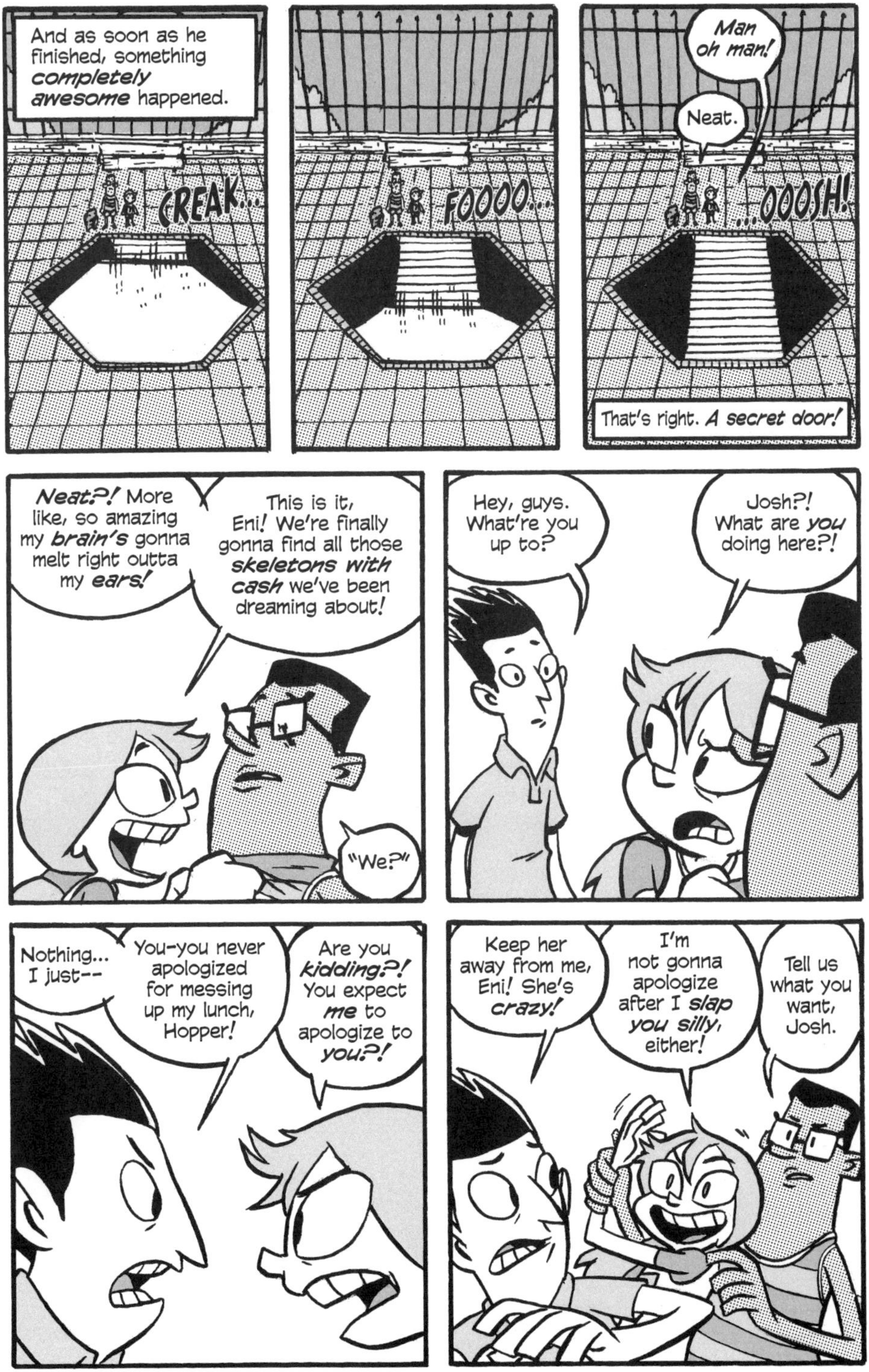
And as soon as he finished, something *completely awesome* happened.
CREAK...
FOOOO...
Man oh man!
Neat.
...OOOSH!
That's right. *A secret door!*
Neat?! More like, so amazing my *brain's* gonna melt right outta my *ears!*
This is it, Eni! We're finally gonna find all those *skeletons with cash* we've been dreaming about!
"We?"
Hey, guys. What're you up to?
Josh?! What are *you* doing here?!
Nothing... I just--
You-you never apologized for messing up my lunch, Hopper!
Are you *kidding?!* You expect *me* to apologize to *you?!*
Keep her away from me, Eni! She's *crazy!*
I'm not gonna apologize after I *slap you silly,* either!
Tell us what you want, Josh.

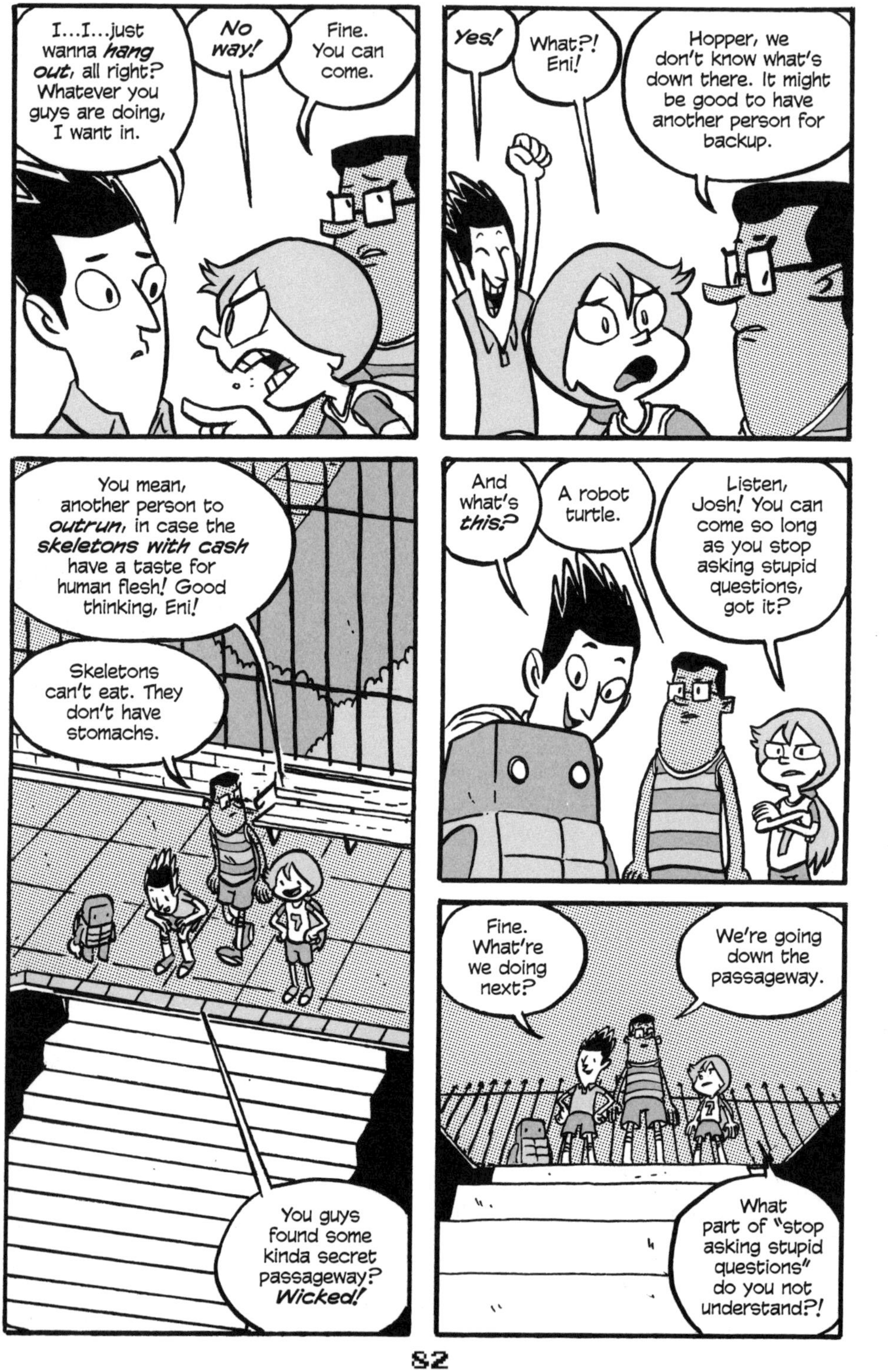
I...I...just wanna *hang out*, all right? Whatever you guys are doing, I want in.
No way!
Fine. You can come.
Yes!
What?! Eni!
Hopper, we don't know what's down there. It might be good to have another person for backup.
You mean, another person to *outrun*, in case the *skeletons with cash* have a taste for human flesh! Good thinking, Eni!
Skeletons can't eat. They don't have stomachs.
You guys found some kinda secret passageway? *Wicked!*
And what's *this?*
A robot turtle.
Listen, Josh! You can come so long as you stop asking stupid questions, got it?
Fine. What're we doing next?
We're going down the passageway.
What part of "stop asking stupid questions" do you not understand?!

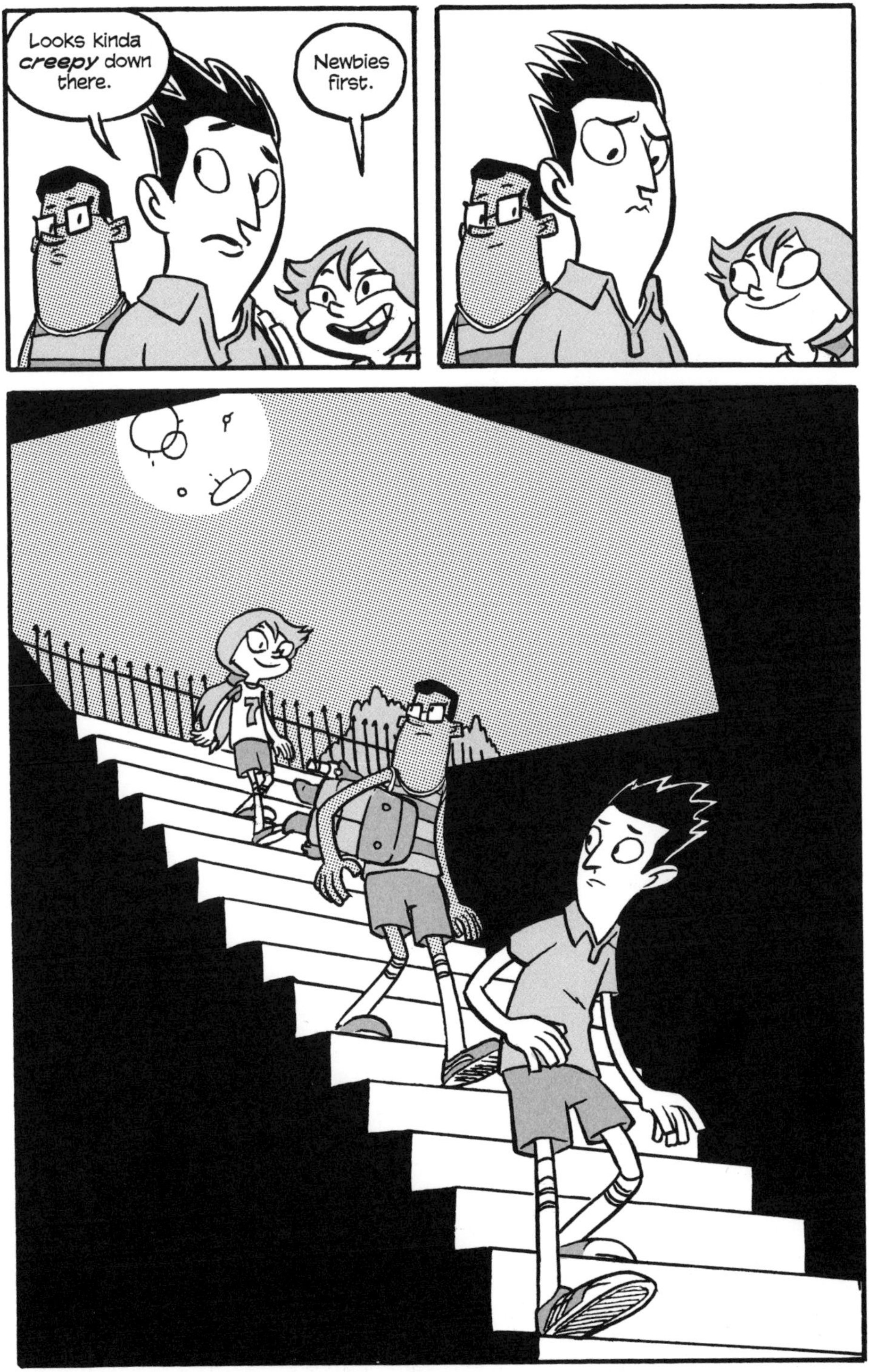
Looks kinda *creepy* down there.
Newbies first.

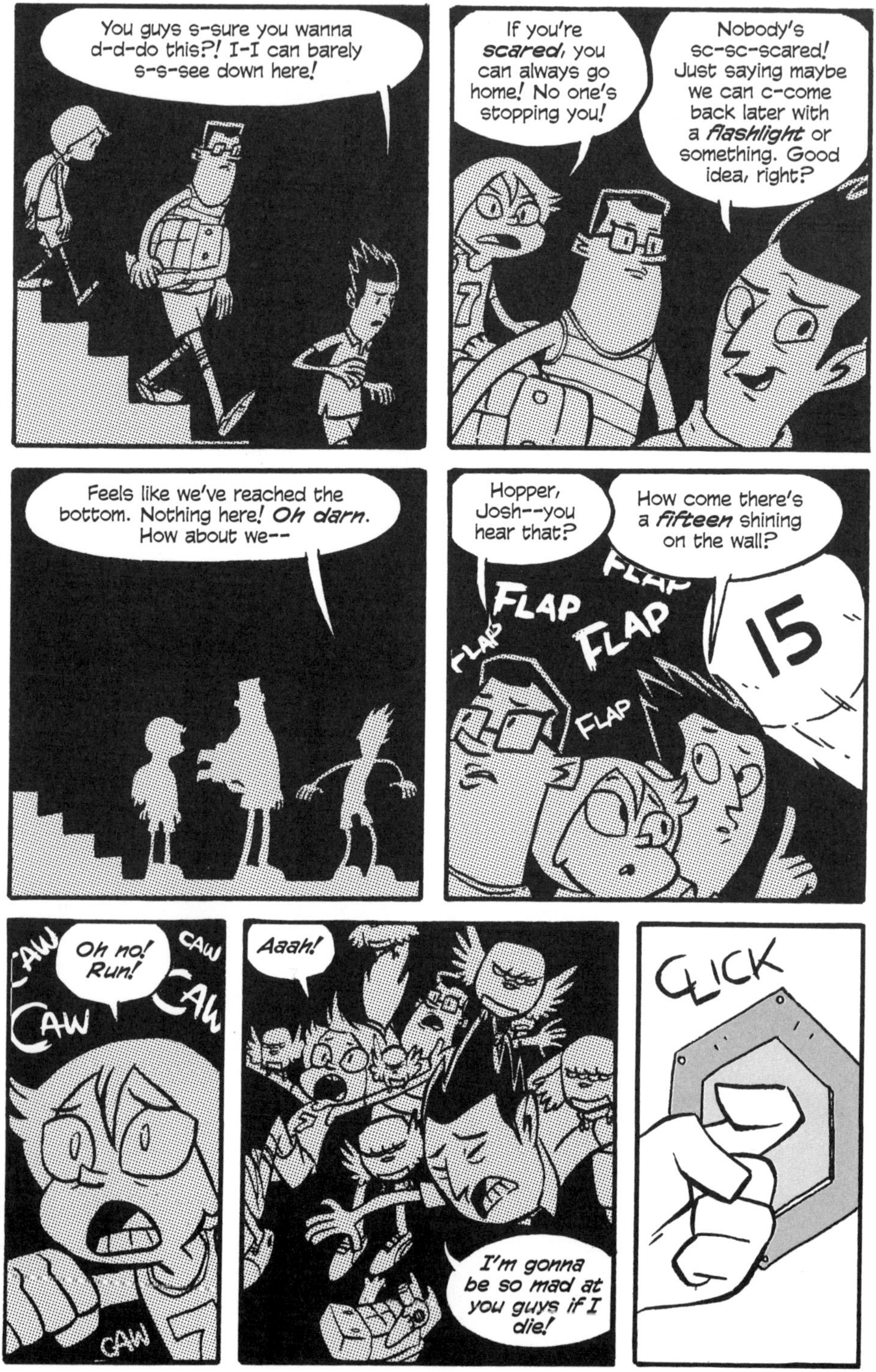
You guys s-sure you wanna d-d-do this?! I-I can barely s-s-see down here!
If you're *scared*, you can always go home! No one's stopping you!
Nobody's sc-sc-scared! Just saying maybe we can c-come back later with a *flashlight* or something. Good idea, right?
Feels like we've reached the bottom. Nothing here! *Oh darn*. How about we--
Hopper, Josh--you hear that?
How come there's a *fifteen* shining on the wall?
FLAP
FLAP
FLAP
FLAP
FLAP
FLAP
15
CAW
Oh no! Run!
CAW
CAW
CAW
CAW
Aaah!
I'm gonna be so mad at you guys if I die!
CLICK

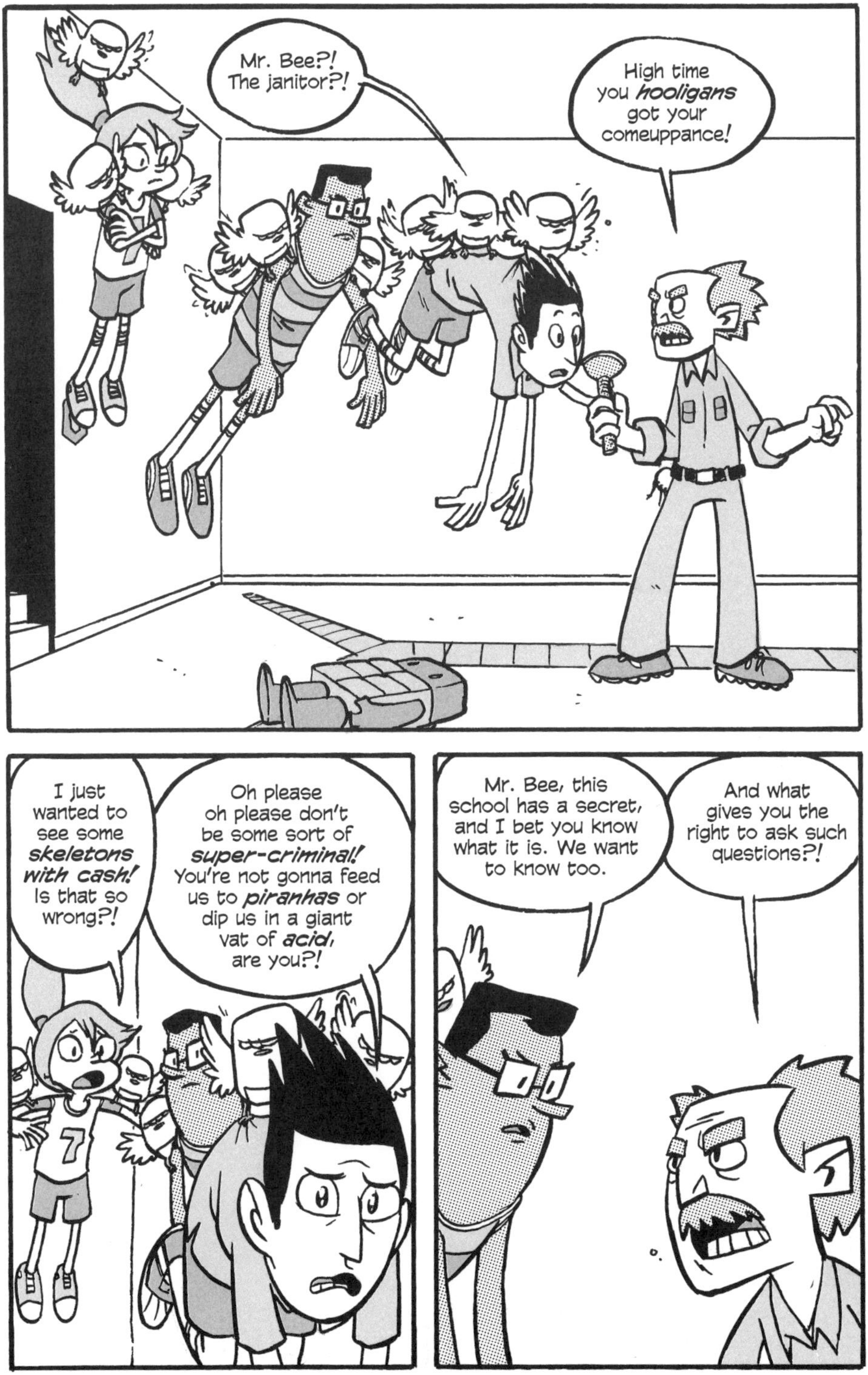
Mr. Bee?! The janitor?!
High time you *hooligans* got your comeuppance!
I just wanted to see some *skeletons with cash!* Is that so wrong?!
Oh please oh please don't be some sort of *super-criminal!* You're not gonna feed us to *piranhas* or dip us in a giant vat of *acid*, are you?!
Mr. Bee, this school has a secret, and I bet you know what it is. We want to know too.
And what gives you the right to ask such questions?!

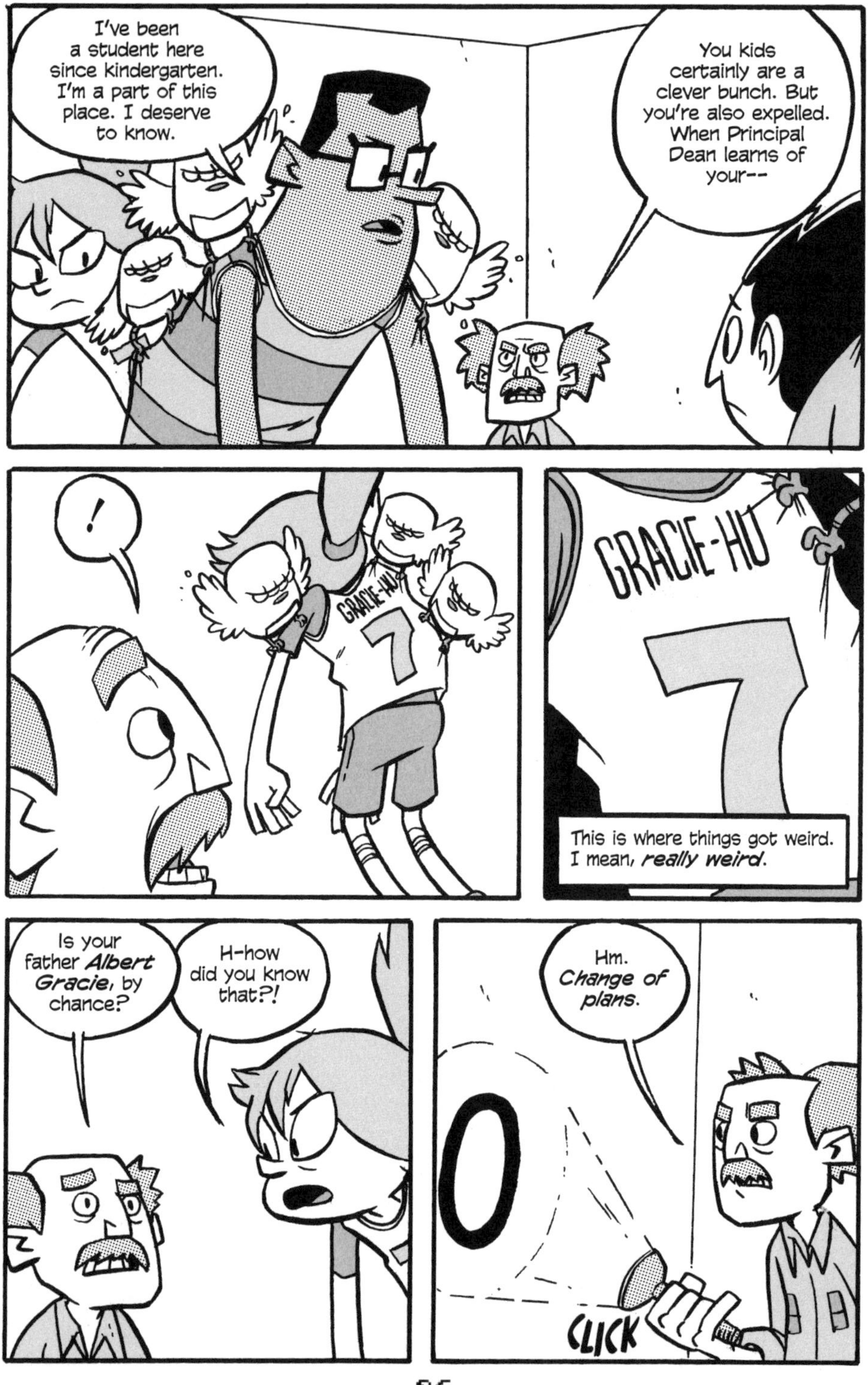
I've been a student here since kindergarten. I'm a part of this place. I deserve to know.
You kids certainly are a clever bunch. But you're also expelled. When Principal Dean learns of your--
!
GRACIE-HU
7
GRACIE-HU
7
This is where things got weird. I mean, *really weird*.
Is your father *Albert Gracie*, by chance?
H-how did you know that?!
Hm. *Change of plans*.
CLICK

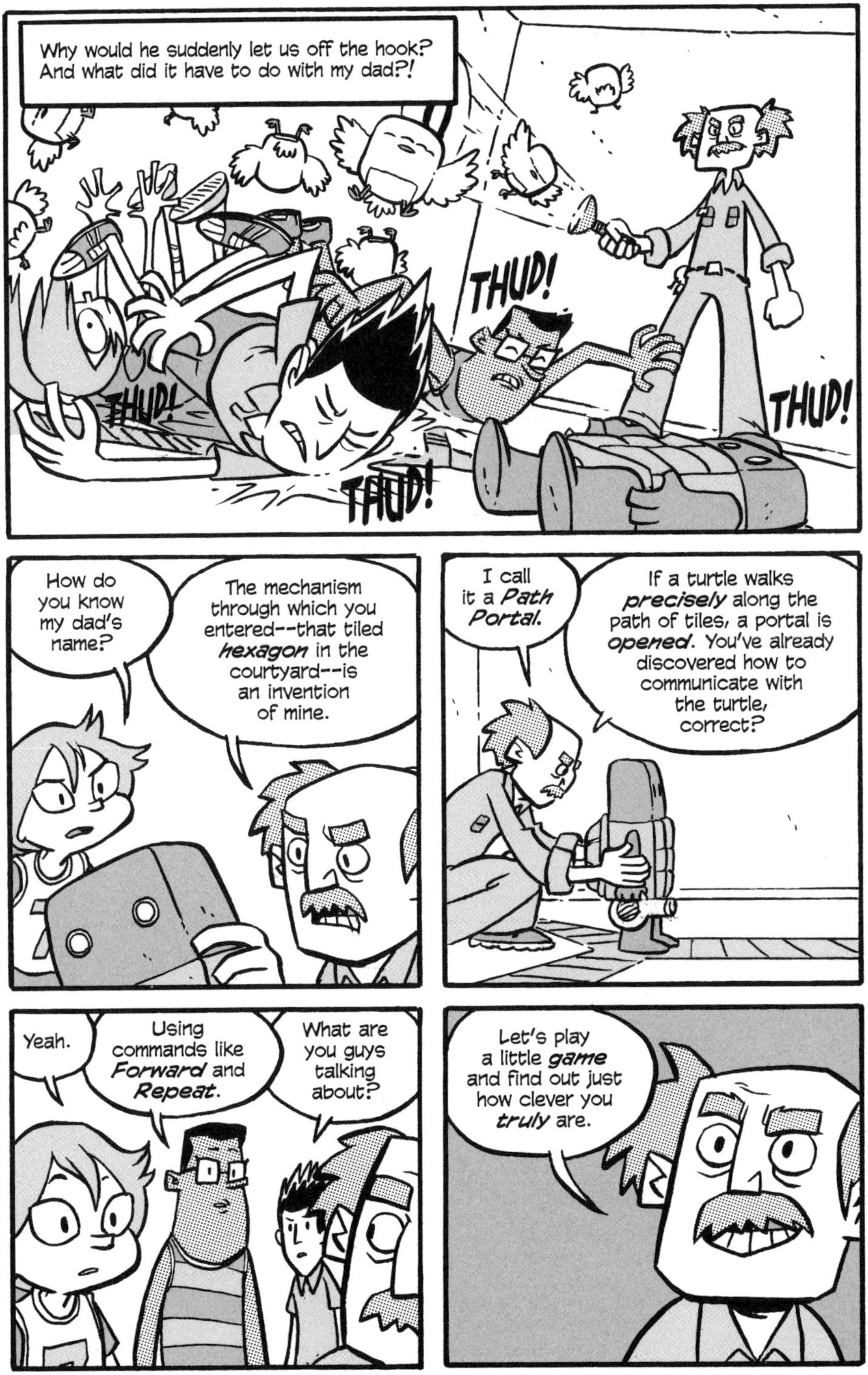
Why would he suddenly let us off the hook? And what did it have to do with my dad?!
THUD!
THUD!
THUD!
THUD!
How do you know my dad's name?
The mechanism through which you entered--that tiled *hexagon* in the courtyard--is an invention of mine.
I call it a *Path Portal.*
If a turtle walks *precisely* along the path of tiles, a portal is *opened*. You've already discovered how to communicate with the turtle, correct?
Yeah.
Using commands like *Forward* and *Repeat*.
What are you guys talking about?
Let's play a little *game* and find out just how clever you *truly* are.

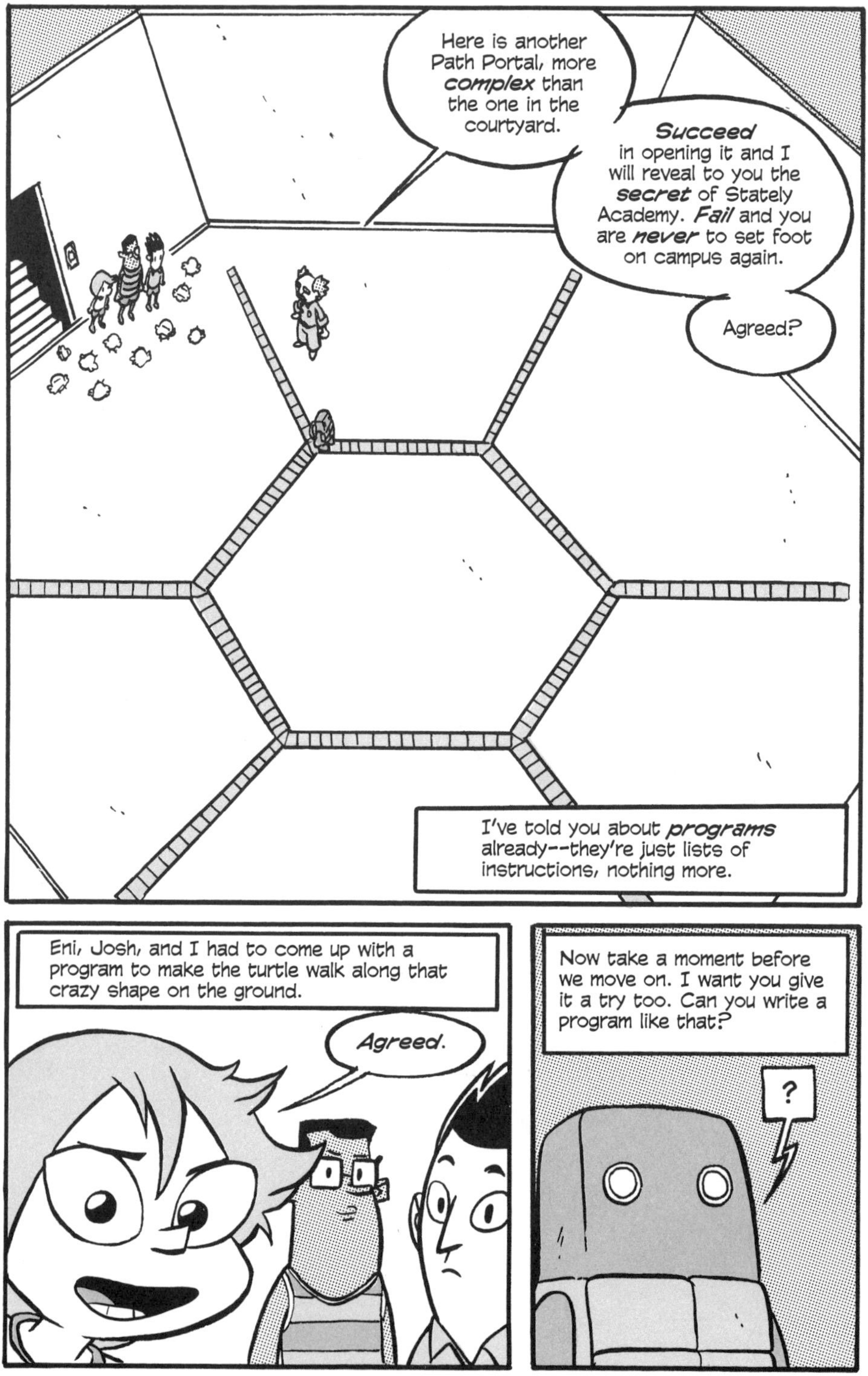
Here is another Path Portal, more *complex* than the one in the courtyard.
Succeed in opening it and I will reveal to you the *secret* of Stately Academy. *Fail* and you are *never* to set foot on campus again.
Agreed?
I've told you about *programs* already--they're just lists of instructions, nothing more.
Eni, Josh, and I had to come up with a program to make the turtle walk along that crazy shape on the ground.
Agreed.
Now take a moment before we move on. I want you give it a try too. Can you write a program like that?
?

GREAT GRAPHIC NOVELS

From the *New York Times*–Bestselling Author
Gene Luen Yang

978-1-59643-152-2

"Gene Luen Yang has created that rare article: a youthful tale with something new to say about American youth."
—*The New York Times*

978-1-59643-359-5   978-1-59643-689-3

"Read this, and come away shaking."
—Gary Schmidt, Newbery Honor–winning author

"A masterful work of historical fiction."
—Dave Eggers, author of
A Heartbreaking Work of Staggering Genius

THE EXCITING NEW SERIES

978-1-62672-075-6

"Brings computer coding to life."
—*Entertainment Weekly*

978-1-59643-697-8

★ "A brilliant homage."
—BCCB

978-1-59643-235-2

"Bravura storytelling."
—*Publishers Weekly*

978-1-59643-156-0

★ "Absolutely not to be missed."
—Booklist

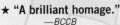

:01
First Second
NEW YORK

Author's Note

It was the summer of 1984, and I'd just finished the fifth grade.

Everybody knows that summers are meant to be fun. You're supposed to goof off at the local swimming pool, or stage epic action figure battles, or watch endless reruns of *Voltron*. You're supposed do whatever you want as long as it doesn't involve school. After all, summer and school are opposites. Not just opposites, mortal enemies. Everybody knows that.

Unfortunately for me, my mom was not "everybody." After two weeks of *Voltron* reruns, she sent me to summer school. I had to take three, maybe four, "enrichment" classes. Now, thirty years later, I only remember one of them: Introduction to Computer Programming.

Our classroom had row after row of computers, more than I'd ever seen in one place. Computers back then weren't what they are today. The only color they displayed was green. They couldn't get on the World Wide Web because it hadn't been invented yet. They stored all their data on these flimsy black disks, and when you stuck a disk into a computer, the sound it made was a cross between a wheeze and a burp.

Even so, computers were magic.

The teacher paired me up with a kid named Bill who was a year older and a head taller. He had this weird habit of cracking his knuckles whenever he was thinking. It was annoying at first, but pretty soon I didn't mind. You see, Bill had coded before. He knew what he was doing.

Even before our first lesson, Bill could make the computer do the most remarkable things. He made it solve math problems, play music, tell jokes. And, most impressive to me at the time, he made it draw.

With just a few commands, Bill could make something intricate and wondrous appear on the screen, something resembling a burst of fireworks, or maybe an alien snowflake. Bill was a magician. I wanted to be one too.

And by the last day of class, I was. I'd learned a few simple commands that could be combined in an infinite number of ways, to accomplish an infinite number of tasks. My parents bought a computer for our family, and I didn't watch another episode of *Voltron* for the rest of that summer.

Coding is creative and powerful. It's how words turn into image and action. It truly is magic. Mike Holmes and I made the book you now hold in your hands because we want to share a bit of that magic with you, and maybe inspire you to become a magician—a coder—yourself.

Happy Coding!

Gene Luen Yang